St

THE
ELEPHANT

Copyright © 2010 Shanghai Press and Publishing Development
Company

This book is edited and designed by the Editorial Committee of
Cultural China series

Managing Directors: Wang Youbu, Xu Naiqing
Editorial Director: Wu Ying
Series Editor: Wang Jiren
Editor: Parker Barnes

Text by Chen Cun
Translation by Yawtsong Lee

Interior and Cover Design: Wang Wei
Cover Image: Getty Images

ISBN: 978-1-60220-217-7

Address any comments about *The Elephant* to:

Better Link Press
99 Park Ave
New York, NY 10016
USA
or
Shanghai Press and Publishing Development Company
F 7 Donghu Road, Shanghai, China (200031)
Email: comments_betterlinkpress@hotmail.com

Printed in China by Shanghai Donnelley Printing Co. Ltd.

1 2 3 4 5 6 7 8 9 10

THE ELEPHANT

By Chen Cun

Better Link Press

Preface

English readers will be presented with a set of 12 pocket books. These books contain 12 outstanding novellas written by 12 writers from Shanghai over the past 30 years. Most of the writers were born in Shanghai from the late 1940's to the late 1950's. They started their literary careers during or after the 1980's. For various reasons, most of them lived and worked in the lowest social strata in other cities or in rural areas for much of their adult lives. As a result they saw much of the world and learned lessons from real life before finally returning to Shanghai. They embarked on their literary careers for various reasons, but most of them were simply passionate about writing. The writers are involved in a variety of occupations, including university professors, literary editors, leaders of literary institutions and professional writers. The diversity of topics covered in these novellas will lead readers to discover the different experiences and motivations of the authors. Readers will encounter a fascinating range of esthetic convictions as they analyze the authors' distinctive artistic skills and writing styles. Generally speaking, a realistic writing style dominates most of their literary works. The literary works they have elaborately created are a true reflection of drastic social changes, as well as differing perspectives towards urban life in Shanghai. Some works created by avant-garde writers have been selected in order to present a variety of styles. No matter what writing styles they adopt though, these writers have enjoyed a definite place, and exerted a positive influence, in Chinese literary circles over the past three decades.

Known as the "Paris of the Orient" around the world, Shanghai was already an international metropolis in the 1920's and 1930's. During that period, Shanghai was China's economic, cultural and literary center. A high number of famous Chinese writers lived, created and published their literary works in Shanghai, including, Lu Xun, Guo Moruo, Mao Dun and Ba Jin. Today, Shanghai has become a globalized metropolis. Writers who have pursued a literary career in the past 30 years are now faced with new challenges and opportunities. I am confident that some of them will produce other fine and influential literary works in the future. I want to make it clear that this set of pocket books does not include all representative Shanghai writers. When the time is ripe, we will introduce more representative writers to readers in the English-speaking world.

Wang Jiren
Series Editor

ONE

Since 1983 or thereabouts I've wanted to write a novel with the title *The Elephant*. Elephants are worth writing about. I started out quite confident that I could do it, thinking that elephants couldn't be more complicated than people. But four years later the novel has yet to be born.

Materials collected for the project, manuscripts representing false starts and half-baked attempts, have languished in my drawers and folders. I am now reviving the Elephant project. Elephants are a hard subject to write about, undoubtedly. Equally unquestionable is my determination to produce an expertly executed work this time. With this in mind I've decided to start off with a discussion of creative writing and peel deeper into the story, layer after layer. It is an unusual opening and has been chosen with a hidden motive.

One day last year, under an overcast sky fresh after a rain, I went to a place formerly known as The China-Soviet Union Friendship Building, now called The Shanghai Exhibition Center. Cracks had appeared in the Building, on the floor. They had been patched up, though the result never looked as good as before. But I digress. What I wanted to talk about was not the Building or Center but a book fair held on its premises in the summer of 1986.

Although it was only a preview of the Fair, it already drew a large crowd. I made the mistake of not riding my bicycle to the exhibition. With a bad back and weak legs, my movements were significantly hampered without the aid of a bicycle. I don't recall whether I had taken my pills that day; but even with the pills I would still be in pain when I walked. I limped toward the exhibition hall, pausing from time to time to placate my hip joints, which were acting up. I ran into a few acquaintances along the way, and after exchanging greetings I waved them along, telling them not to slow down for me. I said I was looking for books about elephants.

An explanation is in order as to how the idea of writing about elephants originally struck me.

With the exception of a thousand-word story *A Nine-year-old Dog*, I had never before used an animal as the main character of a novel. A dog, a cat or a bird fluttering into the air may creep into a story, but only as cameos. More ink perhaps has been expended on dogs than on other animals in my works; I had once even proposed the title of *The Spotted Dog Gali* for the story that eventually was called *The Blue Flag*. The dog title was shot down by a magazine editor who thought it frivolous. I had never written about wild animals, much less wild animals in the wild. I'd never done any bear hunting.

One day I woke up late, as usual, and lay

in bed smoking and gazing at the ceiling, which was quite small, not much larger than an elephant skin fully spread. That brought to mind the image of an elephant and a legend I'd heard as a child.

I felt a stirring in my heart.

The idea of writing about an elephant took hold that very morning. It was a small, dimly lit room, its ceiling stained with yellow rainwater with an eighteen-lumen fluorescent light hanging indolently from it. In the room were four cabinets, a bed, a writing desk, a dining table, and three chairs. All of its three doors opened into the room. I felt my body expand in volume and my skin come into contact with the furniture and the walls, blocking all the doors.

I should be able to write, in this life, a novel with the title *Elephant*, but I was not so sure I could do justice to the subject. I already knew this as I limped toward the book fair. I was just looking for something to occupy myself, to embarrass, and make a fool of myself with an impossible subject.

I didn't find any book on elephants at the book fair. The truth is I had already in my possession multiple books about elephants. A person called Zhong Acheng mailed me a copy of the ninety-page 1982 edition of *Among the Elephants*, published by the Sichuan Publishing House for Children and Adolescents. I also received three books sent by a person by the name of Hong Zi. The book titles were not very impressive; they were *African Animals, Wonders of the African Animal Kingdom* and *Interesting Facts about Rare Animals*, with "Wonders" being the best of the three. There are a total of seventy-five pages in the three books devoted to elephants. 90 + 75 = 165. Armed with 165 pages of information about elephants, it shouldn't be too difficult to write a not too long story about them.

That was what I thought at the time.

That was how I began the aborted story, in which I described the life of one elephant, from his conception to his death. I gave him the name "The Elephant."

I omitted the insemination part and started with the elephant's conception inside his mother's womb, where he felt very bored and useless, with nothing to occupy him. He listened to the sounds and movements both inside and outside his mother's body, trying to guess what was happening.

I knew this did not quite conform to nature. I did not intend to write a children's story or a fable, nor did I want to make the story into a documentary. I really believed my elephant had heard everything. I wanted him to hear everything.

The Elephant continued to float suspended in his mother's womb, and his mother continued to live among her herd. I imagined the setting to be in Africa. Accordingly I watched religiously every episode of the TV series *Africa* and took careful notes. I even recorded the sound tracks. I watched the Oscar-winning movie *Out of Africa*. I saw it last October in Yugoslavia. I didn't find it particularly helpful in furthering my project. The title of that movie in Serbian was literally *My Africa*.

I really didn't need to be such a stickler for the facts. The truth is my Elephant was not conceived by his mother but by me. Strictly speaking, he was the product not of the womb but of the cerebrum, and therefore I should have all the facts about him at my fingertips. I had absolutely no need to mention the names of Acheng or Hong Zi, or to go to a book fair. I had right in front of me a pink plastic elephant, a gift from a friend. It could serve as inspiration for a perfectly good story. I had been so dumb.

Throughout my story, the Elephant was a lonely figure. It was a solitude of the heart. True, he had his mother and his playmates; and he dated when he grew into adulthood, possibly sowing a few wild oats. But none of this helped, he would always feel lonely. This had been preordained when he was cooped up in his mother's womb. Throughout his life he would be struck by a deep terror whenever he thought of that despairing darkness.

Thus began the life of the Elephant.

I'm not done explaining the origin of the idea of writing about elephants, but I don't feel like continuing at this moment. I couldn't wait to get out of the Shanghai Exhibition Center. There were too many people, and the perspiration from so many bodies created a discomfort that could not be relieved by either Coca Cola or electric fans.

I emerged from the exhibition hall with a bunch of books. I paid more than a hundred yuan for a complete set of the Chinese edition of the *Concise Encyclopedia Britannica*. I also bought a *Collection of the World's Paintings of the Human Body*, which was cheaper at twenty-six yuan. Under the weight of the eleven books, every step I took was a struggle. I regretted having left my bicycle at home.

I had to keeping passing the books from one hand to the other every few steps. The thin string that tied the books together tortured my palms and I began to panic, uncertain that I could hold up and make it to the mass transit stop. The pavement being wet from a recent rain, I couldn't rest the books on the ground to catch my breath.

I need to rest my pen at this point. Elephants are oversized animals. As the old saying goes, "It's a big elephant's ass—you can't budge it." So, writing about elephants is tiring and so is watching someone do it.

TWO

Kilimanjaro is a live volcano situated in eastern Africa. At an elevation of 5895 meters, it is the highest peak in Africa. Ernest Hemingway (July 21, 1898–July 2, 1961) managed to write *The Snows of Kilimanjaro* before he blew off half of his head with a shotgun. He starts the story, in type that stands out from the surrounding text, with:

Kilimanjaro is a snow-covered mountain 19,710 feet high, and is said to be the highest mountain in Africa. Its western summit is called the Masai "Ngaje Ngai", the House of God. Close to the western summit there is the dried and frozen carcass of a leopard. No one has explained what the leopard was seeking at that altitude.

My Elephant was neither dried nor frozen. The mother's womb was dark and cosy. The Elephant, in his curled fetal position, listened with frustration to the sounds from inside and outside his mother's body. He tried to break free, squirming and wriggling until he lost his patience and became exhausted.

He could tell when his mother was in motion and when she was stationary. Generally speaking he preferred motion. The bobbing movement imparted a sense of lying on a stretcher.

Finally, one day, his patience was strained to the limit. He began to expand, defying the strong resistance, containment and pressure of the womb, as his skin came into contact with the wall of the uterus.

He felt he was crumpled, crushed and processed into excrement that was squeezed through a long and mean passage. And there was nothing he could do about it. The memory

of this initial humiliation would stay with him
for years.

What an endless darkness!

That overcast afternoon after a recent rain, I
left the Shanghai Exhibition Center carrying
nearly ten thousand pages in eleven 16mo
books. The water jets of the fountain on the
grounds of the Center rose limply and quickly
fell back to ground. The air was heavy with
moisture and heat.

People would occasionally shoot a glance
at me, their eyes aiming low and sweeping
upwards from the most uncivilized part
of my body to rest on my face so that they
could confirm who possessed the body. Then
they briskly walked past me. I was somewhat
indifferent to their gazes. I'd been subjected
to so many of these stares I had no choice but
to become indifferent. I tried my best to walk
with agility and skill. When one has problems
with his back and legs, one has to walk in this
way. Paraphrasing an obscure pamphlet by
Henri Bergson entitled Laughter: *An Essay*

on the Meaning of the Comic, deformities are grimaces of the body. It was an apt and interesting observation. My body thus moved through space with a grimace.

My present narration progresses faster than I walked on that afternoon. The string tying the books together cut into my palms like a knife.

In retrospect, at that time I was not without some premonition of Lin Yi's appearance. I saw her in a dream the previous night, or more correctly, someone resembling her, standing a great distance from me at the foot of an enclosure wall, a colored cloth pinafore over her chest, surrounded by other kids in the kindergarten. In my dream her face did not bear a close resemblance to her present form. She was sucking on her finger. The sun fell on the left side of her face, creating the image of a face with one side contracted and the other relaxed. I tried in the dream to recall her name but without success. Now I knew she must be Lin Yi.

Lin Yi made her way toward me, taking the books from me and putting her arm in mine, without uttering a word.

I felt as if the pain in my hip joints was immediately alleviated.

My legs are not that bad. Of course this would be putting it charitably. What I mean is my legs still serve their purpose provided my hip joints don't act up.

Both of my legs are afflicted, but I can take comfort in the fact that they have never acted up at the same time. This is only fair; it is unreasonable to incapacitate both legs of a person at the same time. My real problem is with my back or the small of my back. It started over ten years ago, when I was a peasant in the countryside. Back then Lin Lin and I were together.

I'd never liked planting seedlings or harvesting rice; I hated any work that required bending at the waist. So I mainly hauled stuff in two baskets balanced on a pole on my shoulder—fifty to one hundred fifty pounds at a time. When I toted stuff on my shoulder, Lin Lin would normally be working in the fields with her back bent low.

Thinking back, it was after a night of battling with Lin Lin that I felt an unprecedented pain in my back. It was not the first time my back gave me trouble; only, the intensity of the pain I felt on that occasion was three times greater than before. I told her I couldn't do it; I remember saying I was sorry. She sat up under the mosquito netting, told me to continue to lie on my stomach and started kneading and rubbing the small of my back with medium pressure, causing me to moan with pain. That night I braved the pain and managed to finish what I'd started. I was beginning to feel like a man.

Under the mosquito net, she knelt by me, kneading and rubbing away, her clothes bunched up at my feet with a button pressed into one of them. I did not look over my shoulder at her. At daybreak, beads of sweat dripped down to the small of my back, along her arms, then flowed across my weak back muscles onto the bed.

Daylight crept through the cracks in the

adobe wall and fell onto the mosquito net, picking out the mosquitoes made anemic by a night of anxious, futile waiting outside the mesh. Lin Lin finally said she was exhausted and flopped down on my back with her arms limp and full weight on me. Our sweat mingled. Her perspiring chest and belly felt surprisingly cool against my back. We lay in that position until I couldn't support her weight anymore and I felt it was time to finish what I had set out to do.

When Lin Lin and I were locked in battle, Lin Yi was still a kid. The first time I saw her she was in primary school—the previous scene of her kindergarten days was a figment of my imagination. At that time Lin Yi always called me uncle, which annoyed Lin Lin to no end. I often held Lin Yi on my knees and wove stories for her. I should clarify that I never kissed her then. She was by that time already a big kid, so it would have been inappropriate for her to be kissed by a man. It was only years later that I kissed her, when she was older, and a kiss from a man became appropriate.

With Lin Yi taking the books off my hands, I no longer limped but still walked slowly. We got on and off public transportation. She escorted me to my door. When I invited her to come in for a brief visit, she declined.

I didn't insist after she declined two times. I took the books from her and gave her a pat on the forehead. Then I went upstairs alone.

THREE

I reread the story I'd just written. I felt that if it ended with "I went upstairs alone," it would be a nice little story. This story of mine can be ended where I choose.

Of course it doesn't have to end anywhere.

Suppose the story did not end here and I was walking up the stairs. My home is on the third floor and there is no elevator in the building. After going up thirty-nine steps, I began fishing for my keys. I could not find them. I tried to remember but came up blank. So I took two steps back and kicked the door with a vengeance. It opened. My knees buckled and I landed on my buttocks, all eleven books in my hand flying in different directions as they hit the floor.

All eleven books were beautifully made.

I stepped out that day to deal with some trivial matter and missed the moment of my Elephant's birth. When I hurried home, he had already been born. Based on the observations of Iain and Oria Douglas-Hamilton, British co-authors of *Among the Elephants*, my Elephant would at this moment be standing under his mother's belly, wet and dripping with blood, and the mother's hind legs and trunk would be smeared with blood. The two big female elephants who midwived the birth would also have blood on their trunks. My Elephant emerged from darkness only to be surrounded by a sea of red. The Elephant was born at midday. His mother, about thirteen years old, her strength drained, her head hanging low, and her legs bent, was exhausted and showed no interest in my Elephant.

Enough of quoting from someone else's

book. The Douglas-Hamiltons have had their say. Now it's my turn.

Allow me, however, one last quote from their book, a minor detail. My elephant curled his trunk upward and downward, looking for milk. The mother elephant's breasts, in number, position, shape and size, are similar to a human female's. The breasts develop fully after the first pregnancy and start producing milk for life. My Elephant was now learning how to suckle. This is also part of animal instinct.

The glum-looking mother elephant suddenly kicked up her powerful and strong hind leg, hit the Elephant on his head and sent him tumbling into the tall grass.

He gave up all hope, reduced to gazing despondently after the two breasts before his eyes.

Another female elephant, flat-chested, walked over to him, opening her front legs and pulling the Elephant with her trunk toward her. Tenderly and affectionately she caressed his head with her trunk.

The Elephant, reassured, calmed down. He

would remain grateful all his life to this female that provided protection and care in the first hours of his life. In due time, he would repay the kindness with his body. The snow-capped Kilimanjaro rose majestically in the distance.

With the birth of the Elephant out of the way, I can now give an unhurried account of how I conceived of this story.

As I mentioned before, it was on a morning in 1983 that the idea of writing about an elephant first came to me, when I recalled a legend about elephants. It was a well known tale about the elephant graveyards which existed in areas inhabited by herds of elephants. Generations of aging elephants, answering God's summons, had of their own accord left their herds, alone, to find the graveyards, guided by a mysterious instinct. And after long treks over mountains and across rivers, they lay down quietly among the skeletons of their ancestors and brethren to await death. No humans have ever been able to find these elephant graveyards, so full of treasured tusks.

That was what flashed through my mind that morning.

What moved me was the aging elephants separated themselves from their herd, their solitary trek and the final, silent wait in prostration. The image filled me with emotion.

I know the legend stands on shaky ground. No one has ever seen an elephant graveyard. Scientists point out that the gathering of a large number of elephant skeletons in one place could easily be explained by the wildfires that rage unchecked across the African savanna. Generally speaking, science is a wet blanket. Science is also often just a perfect excuse for laziness. I know these graveyards exist; failure to find one doesn't mean they don't exist. People are more objective in other matters (such as in matters of love); they don't automatically conclude from the fact that they have failed to find a suitable mate that such mates cannot possibly exist. Without the graveyards, *The Elephant* wouldn't have existed. Since *The Elephant* does exist, the existence of the elephant graveyards is indisputable.

In this emotional account, I will try not to dwell excessively on the question of existence or non-existence of something or another. It was in this spirit that I followed the footprints of elephants to the graveyard. In that wood, countless skeletons of elephants lay strewn about: bleached bones picked clean of muscle and skin, and hotly sought-after tusks, in abundance and for the picking. I bent down to fondly caress the elephant tusks, tusks that were almost warm to the touch. The huge skulls stared fiercely at the intruder with their abysmal eyes, and I, the intruder, stared back at the black holes in the skulls, imagining their past glory. Those long lashes, the envy of beauty-conscious females anywhere, were long gone.

A snake came out of a black hole.

There were snakes all over the place.

In fact I spent that afternoon with Lin Yi. At the entrance of the building I did not invite her in, nor did she decline the invitation not issued. She walked ahead of me, with the heavy bundle of books dangling from her hand. After ascending thirty-nine steps, she was panting. With a hand on the wall for support, I walked up step by breathless step, bringing up the rear. My joints were in excruciating pain again.

She got out the keys from her skirt pocket, opened the door, turned on the light and walked in without waiting for me.

How and where she had obtained the keys has remained a mystery to this day. I felt my pocket and found my keys were still where they ought to be.

By the time I entered my apartment, the books had been placed on the bed with the string undone. Lin Yi was sitting on the edge of the bed, head lowered and eyes on the string, which she was coiling up neatly for future use. I closed the door after me and she passed me the coiled string, while turning on the radio cassette recorder on my desk with the other hand. The volume was high and after bearing with it for a few seconds she turned it down.

We filled the remainder of the day with

numerous activities. The first was reading. She read the *Collection of the World's Paintings of the Human Body,* while I read the *Concise Encyclopedia Britannica.* She had a curious way of looking at the paintings, first the ones in color, then the black and white, and finally returning to the color ones. Examining the spines of the books, I selected Volume 8, whose entries go from "tu" to "ye." On page 556 I found the entry about elephants. If the reader is uninterested in this information, please feel free to skip these thousand words. The reader is free to skip over any number of words anywhere within this story.

Elephant: the largest living land animal of the order Proboscidea and the family Elephantidae, characterized by its long trunk, columnar legs, and huge head with temporal glands and wide, flat ears. Elephants are grayish to brown in color, and their body hair is sparse and coarse. Both the Indian (Asian) elephant (*Elephas maximus*) and the African elephant (*Loxodonta africana*) possess tusks and elongating incisors, whereas in the Asian elephant it is mainly the male that has tusks. The

nostrils are located at the tip of the flexible trunk;
at the end of the trunk are finger-like projections
enabling it to pick up small objects. Elephants
drink by sucking water into the trunk and then
squirting it into the mouth. Male elephants do
not have scrota and their testicles are housed
internally. The African elephant, the largest living
land animal, weighs up to 7,500 kg and stands 3
to 4 meters at the shoulder. The Asian elephant
weighs about 5,000 kg and has a shoulder height
of up to 2.5 ~ 3 meters. African elephants have
much larger ears. Elephants have six sets of molars
and premolars in their lifetime, but they do not
grow all at once. New teeth develop as worn teeth
break up. The sixth and the last molars will be
worn down after about 60 years of age. Sometimes
tooth loss can be a cause of death, as it brings
on starvation. Therefore few elephants survive
beyond the age of 60. Indian elephants inhabit the
Indian peninsula and Southeast Asia while African
elephants are found only south of the Sahara.
The common belief that there existed "pygmy"
elephants is unfounded; they are probably simply
smaller varieties of the African elephants. Both
species live in lush jungles or treeless tropical
savannas. Elephants live in small family groups

led by old females (cows). Where food is plentiful, the groups join together. Most males (bulls) live in bachelor herds apart from the cows. Elephants migrate seasonally according to the availability of food and water. In a single day, they spend hours eating grass and other plants, often consuming over 225 kg. The average gestation period is 610 days for an Indian elephant and two months longer for an African elephant. The reproductive age starts between 8 ~ 12 years of age for the Indian elephants and about 14 for the African.

As I was reading the entry about elephants, Lin Yi told me that her book contained a hundred color paintings of the human body. Then she asked me an odd question: Why do painters seem to shun pregnant nudes? I gave it some thought without finding an answer. She asked if the painters preferred "unencumbered" women, not wishing to "paint one and get one free?" Such a profound question stumped me even more than the previous one. I said pregnancy was a mysterious thing. She glanced at me and returned to her book, falling silent.

For a long while her eyes were fixed on the

painting *The Death of Marat* by Jacques-Louis David.

For many centuries the Asian elephant has been important as a ceremonial and draft animal. Commanded by its mahout, the elephant was once a fundamental part of Southeast Asian logging operations. Although African elephants have been used as draft animals, the practice is not widespread; they have never been truly tamed since elephants can learn complex tasks only after the age of 20. The capture and training of young elephants require the help of tamed adult elephants. Over many years, this has had the effect of thinning the elephant population. Threatened by habitat loss and human encroachment, elephants are in extreme danger. The Asian elephants have been listed as an endangered species and the number of African elephants has been on the decline, due in large part to poaching. However, in some parts of Africa an overabundance of elephants also has caused further habitat loss. Conservation measures have been taken to address the problem, including the prevention of poaching and the establishment of large wildlife reserves (including major migration corridors). However despite these efforts, culling is still needed in some reserves to prevent habitat destruction.

There! I've finally finished copying this long paragraph. It will be the basis for my story *The Elephant*. Armed with this paragraph, anyone can make up a story.

But the first impression I got when I read the paragraph was that there might have been a mistranslation. The judgmental "in extreme danger" seemed to me to lack grounding in facts. It is true that the population of elephants is declining, but so is the population of certain European countries, and that does not give us the right to say their populations are "in extreme danger." The use of the expression "extreme" is unfortunate. I hasten to add that I in no way encourage poaching. The noble animal that is the elephant fills me with respect and awe. I even found the expression "draft animal" repulsive.

I promise this will be the last quotation from the encyclopedia. It's a much shorter one. After this I will put the encyclopedia back on the shelf. This entry is about ivory.

Ivory: the variety of dentin of which the
tusk of the elephant is composed, prized for its
beauty, durability, and suitability for carving. The
tusk is the upper incisor and continues to grow
throughout the lifetime of the male and female
African elephant and of the male Indian elephant;
the female Indian elephant has no tusks or at most
very small ones. The teeth of the hippopotamus,
walrus, narwhal, sperm whale, and some types
of wild boar and warthog are recognized as ivory
but have little commercial value because of their
small size. Elephant tusks from Africa average
about 6 feet (2 m) in length and weigh about 50
pounds (23 kg) each; tusks from Asian elephants
are somewhat smaller ... There are two main types
of elephant ivory, hard and soft.

After reading this entry, I asked Lin Yi to
stop perusing her album of paintings and pay
attention to me. I told her that even a prestigious
encyclopedia such as this was not immune
to errors in translation. The first sentence of
the entry (in Chinese translation) was clearly

missing a comma or a slight-pause mark. And why did it say "a pair" of elephants? I suspected that the correct translation should be "a pair of tusks of African elephants," instead of "tusks of a pair of African elephants." (Translator's note: there is no error in the original English entry. The expression "a pair of" exists only in the Chinese edition.) After hearing me out, Lin Yi told me to quit being so pedantic and hair-splitting. After a brief pause during which she ran her hand across *The Death of Marat*, she told me her name was Lin Yi and that she was Lin Lin's sister. I couldn't recall Lin Lin having a sister. The earlier scene in the story, with me holding her sister on my knees and making up stories for her, was a pure invention on my part. I probably did have that dream I mentioned, but I knew for a fact that Lin Lin didn't have a sister. Lin Lin got transferred back to Shanghai precisely on the grounds that she was an only child. And the bureaucracies in charge of household registration rarely make mistakes in these matters. Neighbors are notorious for their eagerness to denounce any suspected irregularities.

I asked her again and she said unequivocally she was the sister, not a maternal or paternal cousin, but a blood sister of Lin Lin.

That afternoon when Lin Yi came up to me and took the hefty books off my hand and put her arm through mine, I didn't hesitate even for a second, as if I had been expecting her. She was a spitting image of Lin Lin, except ten years younger.

"Yes, I've been here before," she said.

FOUR

On page 558 of Volume VIII of the encyclopedia I found an entry about Ganesha, a god with the head of an elephant. According to the encyclopedia, sculptures of Ganesha are often found at the entrances of temples and dwellings. There was a picture on the next page of the elephant-headed god, which I studied for a long while. In the early winter of 1982, I went to Chengde and discovered that one of the Eight Outer Temples was guarded by stone elephants instead of the usual stone lions. A photo taken of myself with the stone elephants can no longer be found, perhaps because I never had the roll of film developed after returning from the trip. Ganesha, with the head of an elephant and body of a human, is a Hindu god, son of Shiva and Parvati, and according to legend, he is the remover of obstacles. The stone elephants I saw in front of the temple in Chengde had an elephant head and an elephant body. There was no transmogrification. So apparently they were unrelated to Ganesha.

I was accompanied by Lin Lin on that trip to Chengde. We were already through with each other at that time, but since she had promised to make the trip before our breakup, she came along. While in Chengde and on our way back, we were very civil to each other. I proposed that we sleep in separate hotel rooms, but she did not agree. We ended up sleeping in separate beds in the same room. They were single plank beds. If the two single beds were lined up to make one bed, it would sleep two comfortably. But we didn't do it. During those few days she looked more beautiful than ever; her eyes had dark rings around them, natural, not mascara dark. Only one time did she get up in the middle of the night to urinate in the chamber pot behind the beds in the dark, making a loud splash. She emptied the pot before daybreak. I heard everything, being unable to sleep any of those nights.

It snowed every day while we were in Chengde.

After taking pictures in front of the stone elephants, we entered the Imperial Summer Resort, which had only a few visitors. Lakes hardly held my interest. Lakes are treasured in the north because there aren't many of them there. No matter what lake, be it Lake Kunmin, Lake Daming or any of the those in the Imperial Summer Resort of Chengde, none of them interested me. But the mountains in the north are magnificent. In the hours before sunset, I watched the mountains, including the famous Bangchui (Wooden Club) Peak rising above the surrounding hills until it became too much for me. I turned to look for Lin Lin and found her watching a range of arid hills.

"Hills like white elephants," she observed.

The idea of writing a story about elephants

had not yet entered my mind at that time. I decided to undertake such a project years later. I joined her in her mountain-gazing and found that the hills truly resembled white elephants. Ernest Hemingway did not lie.

Those days it snowed without interruption. The next day when we returned to the Eight Outer Temples, it was still snowing. That day we saw the two-body statue of Samvara.

For some reason that day I couldn't charge the flash on my camera, no matter what I did, and so I was reduced to taking interior pictures by the light reflected off the snow. I used a roll of ASA 100 film, and set the aperture at 2. Leaning against the wall and holding my breath, I took pictures at a shutter speed of one quarter of a second. I kept the camera pressed against my forehead and my arms close against my body, and made sure I pushed the shutter with a smooth, steady movement of my finger. I also tried a shutter speed of one second. As long as I did not exceed 6, the picture quality would be good enough to fool a layman. I have no way of knowing how those pictures turned out; I can't even find those rolls of film.

So Samvara was no different from the rest of us. The idea that Buddhist deities also engaged in sexual intercourse really tickled me. I consulted the *Qing Chao Ye Shi Da Quan (A Nonofficial History of the Qing Dynasty)* and found an entry on the Samvara statues. According to the entry, a worryingly low fertility rate at the time led to the commissioning of the Buddhist statues to set an example. It was meant to show that worldly concerns were also the Buddha's concerns and Buddhist deities shared in human desire. The goal was for the populace to copulate and populate with a vengeance. The statues were lifelike and seemed to be in the middle of an act of song and dance; one of them resembled a modern-day ballet duet on ice. The formidable privates of the Buddhist deity were hidden behind a yellow silk "fig leaf." When I tried to lift the silk cloth to have a closer look, the docent nearby waved his hand without uttering a word, and I gave up. I turned around to look for Lin Lin only to find her already standing outside in the snow.

In the evening we sat on our own bed in the hotel, each wrapped in a quilt to keep warm. I mentioned my disappointment earlier in the day. Lin Lin offered some perspective, observing that overpopulation was the problem now and free-flowing knowledge and information had eliminated the need for the Buddha's demonstration. I explained to her my pursuit of art. With a sneering laugh, she asked me, then what about your own yellow silk "fig leaf"? I had no answer to that.

Surely she wasn't hinting at anything? It must have been a simple retort. She knew we were done, with or without a yellow silk "fig leaf." It could of course be something very casual—just some physical activity to ward off the cold, say. That would have worked. Take the example of the elephants I'm going to write about. They are very casual about this kind of thing. But there was to be no physical exertion; we were not in the mood for physical exercise.

That night I didn't get much sleep. With a strong aversion to sleeping pills, I stoically faced my insomnia, merely closing my eyes to recoup my energy. In the middle of the night my serenity was shattered by the loud singing of torrential urination into a chamber pot. At first light, I finally drifted to sleep but was soon woken up by the almost solar heat of the duct under my pillow. The hotel had just turned on the heat.

The next day Lin Lin and I took the train home. Soon the Samvara statues were forgotten along with the two stone elephants. For good measure, I tried to forget Lin Lin as well.

A long time ago I saw a film *The Capture of an Elephant*. The young elephant captured was called "Banna." The shots of the magnificent natural landscape of Xishuangbanna in the film were captivating. It showed in theaters when the Gang of Four was still in power. Soon word spread that elephants had died or been injured while they were being captured, and the wounded elephants took their vengeance by wreaking havoc on farm land and property, and by attacking humans. The anger of the elephants caused a lot of grief among the local inhabitants. Banna was a female Indian elephant. I'd seen her before. The elephant trappers went to great lengths to capture her. The Chinese traditionally are not elephant trappers. The trapping process consists of first setting traps, into which men lure young elephants. Elephants are good climbers, even on steep slopes, so long as they are not forced to climb up vertical cliffs. The young elephants that have fallen into the trap are left there for a number of days until they become docile. The trappers light bonfires around the rim of the pit and keep vigil, throwing food to the elephants. When they think the time is ripe, they bind the young elephant's leg with cow tendon to a previously tamed adult elephant which drags it back to the village. Once in the village the calf is tied to a big tree trunk and made to learn to obey instructions. If the calf fails to follow an instruction, the already tamed elephants (elephant collaborators?) will smack it with their trunks until its skin becomes raw and tender, and then people step up and pour saltwater on the raw skin.

It's no way to treat a human being, or an elephant for that matter. I don't know if Banna ever received the saltwater treatment. Anyway, Banna was captured and taken to Shanghai, where it was placed in a huge cage—the Elephant Palace.

They only try to tame young elephants. The grown-ups are confirmed savages, with a set *weltanschauung* and therefore incorrigible.

My Elephant was still in the woods, in the wild. People rarely try to domesticate African elephants. Fate had prepared two scenarios for it: either it would continue to live, or it would be killed by some poacher; but it would never become a "running elephant" in the sense of "running dogs," at the beck and call of human masters. Yet its risk of being killed was for now minimal since its tusks were not yet pretty enough.

The Elephant could now feed at its mother's breast. Swinging his trunk out of the way, he suckled with his head turned up.

He was afraid of the dark.

At night Kilimanjaro became a dark shadow, its snow-capped peak a blur. He found he was a little near-sighted, not knowing that all elephants are myopic. The moon was a yellow disk in their eyes. The elephants made a strange trumpeting sound while they raised their trunks to the moon in the sky, as if in worship. Raise it, my child, raise your trunk. The mother's trunk nudged the Elephant's clumsy young trunk toward the sky. Raise it, child, the moon is full. Raise your trunk to the moon.

He raised his trunk in the air and waved it to the right and to the left. A forest of trunks was formed in the woods. The moon cast a soft light on his trunk; he could smell the clean and fresh breath of the moon. The orange yellow disk of light left an indelible mark in the depth of his eyes.

The elephants emitted a low roar.

A crocodile crawled ashore, which was out of character for it, and walked on its four strong limbs, with its body raised off the ground. After creeping a distance, it reared its head, took one look at the herd of stationary elephants and started trotting off like a horse along the water's edge. At nightfall the crocodiles stayed in the river in droves, submerged at the bottom. All was quiet on the waterfront.

The Elephant was bothered by the dark. He now realized that his herd was invincible and there was no need to worry about safety or food. He wanted to grow up as fast as possible so that he could philosophize, unlike those other animals, who were so caught up in the rat race that they had no time for intellectual development. But it would have to wait. Right at this moment he was still suckling at his mother's nipple, which was much like a human's. And it did not dispense philosophy.

The Elephant watched a gorilla build its sleeping nest. He tried to do the same with his trunk but couldn't reach that high. The moon had been hidden by clouds and a more desperate note crept into the elephant herd's howling. He was in no mood for prayers. A fear of the dark originating in the womb expanded and spread until it gradually swallowed the woods and savannas it encountered.

Mournfully he raised his trunk to the sky, toward the moon now obscured by clouds.

FIVE

That evening Lin Yi prepared supper. Saying that cooking would ruin her skirt, she took it off. With false modesty I turned away to flip through the album of paintings while she took off her skirt. I looked at the bathing women of Degas, as if through a window fogged up by moisture. The wet, glistening backs had a strange charm. Lin Yi walked out from behind me and the first thing that entered my field of vision was an exquisite young leg in motion. "Turn around! I'm afraid you'll be disappointed." She flashed a smile at me before turning to start supper.

She had on a pair of white Western-style shorts, which were all the rage at the time. Young girls and boys sporting these white affairs, like clouds hovering at their midriffs, were painting the town "white." But nobody wore them under a skirt like Lin Yi did.

Both at the dining table and in bed, I asked her about Lin Lin's whereabouts. She claimed ignorance, saying to me, there's no longer a Lin Lin, just pretend I'm Lin Lin. I suspected she was deliberately putting me on and told her so. She looked me up and down in contempt. "I didn't expect you to be so conventional." "Well," I said, "I am conventional in a sense. I need to know the past." "Don't I have a past?" she mumbled to herself. She scraped the leftover bones on the table into her bowl and put it away. She made her way to the window, where she shed a few quiet tears with her head supported between her hands.

I went up to her and handed her the skirt.

Taking the skirt from me, she carefully folded it and placed it on the desk. She got to her feet and pulled off her sweatshirt over her head, stripping to her bra. Turning her back to me, she said, unbutton it. She said: you are not stupid. She said leave me alone for a while.

After hearing these words, I did not leave the room. "This time you must leave the room," Lin Yi said.

I did not want to.

I tucked Lin Yi in comfortably before settling down next to her. She rested her pretty little head on my shoulder, as Lin Lin used to do.

"Lin Lin liked to use you as her pillow."

"Yes."

"Lin Yi on the other hand prefers to be your pillow."

So I rested my head on her. It felt good too. She gently patted my back, like the mother elephant trying to coax the calf to sleep. I was no longer a calf and I refused to fall asleep. I sensed the subtle differences between Lin Lin and Lin Yi.

"Lin Lin didn't want me to imitate her."

She tried to calm me down with her hand; she used her left hand. But her attempt at comforting me had the opposite effect. Before long we lost our calm; it returned only after a while. Either way it was fine.

"Take a closer look at me. Are you sure you know me?" Lin Yi said with a half smile.

She looked vaguely familiar. I wanted to get off the bed.

"Don't go."

I got scared. I thought I had probably fallen into a trap a la *Strange Tales from a Chinese Studio*. I was terrified of an evil spirit draped in painted human skin, as in one of the ghost stories in the collection mentioned earlier. I dashed hell-bent toward the door, forgetting that my legs were no longer in running form. A flash of excruciating pain shot through my joints, my legs suddenly got soft under me and I fell near the door.

My hip joints severely limited my mobility. Before every venture out of the house I never failed to do a mental calculation of how far I would need to hoof it. The fortunes of my troublesome joints waxed and waned like the moon. When fortune smiled on me, I could, with effort, keep up with a person walking at a normal pace. But self-satisfaction is often premature. I never knew when I'd be hit by a bolt from the blue and my legs would buckle uncontrollably. So I had learned to remain motionless for a few moments from time to time. I tried not to push them. I took special care when I crossed the street. Dying in the middle of the street would be a nuisance for public sanitation.

I did not often fall. Falling was for the healthy-jointed. Once you had bad legs, your would focus your attention on your legs, and that significantly reduced your chances of falling. But I did have one bad experience. It happened when I was on a bicycle; I felt healthy when I was riding a bike. The day it happened I was riding my bike to the zoo, with a referral letter in hand, to find out more about elephants. It was a cold day and I tried to put on my gloves while riding the bike. First I let go of one hand and then I took the other hand off the handlebar. I had had so much practice riding "hands free." As a result of this over-confidence I fell off the bike, tearing my pants in the process.

I lay on the ground, reluctant to get up. The gravel pressing against my body did not hurt me since I was wearing a padded cotton jacket.

I placed blame partially on the elephants. Were it not for them, I wouldn't have taken such a humiliating fall. When I saw a group of girls heading my way I quickly picked myself up and righted the handlebar knocked askew by the fall. I continued riding toward the zoo. Chastened by the fall, I kept both hands on the handlebar, banishing all thoughts of showing off my skills.

The zoo brimmed with activity. There were more visitors than animals. When I showed my referral letter to the gate guard I was admitted, together with my bike, free of charge. I already felt much better.

I waited on my feet in front of the Elephant Palace. Amid the stench stood three adult elephants and one calf, looking bored to death.

The adults each had chains attached to their legs.

The person who received me watched me with a vigilant eye, because I told him I'd seen the film *The Capture of an Elephant*. They had had quite enough of the endless tongue-wagging triggered by the capture of an elephant. I explained that I was not trying to capture any anecdotes about the captors of the elephant. I was there to learn more about elephants' traits and behaviors. After making a phone call, he told me to pay a visit to the Elephant Palace. When I asked about scientific research, he said there was none conducted at the zoo. He didn't even know the height and weight of the elephants at the zoo. It immediately brought to mind the story about the ingenious idea of Cao Chong (the young son of famous historical figure Cao Cao) for finding out the weight of a big elephant.

The young zookeeper in charge of the elephants had worked there for ten years. He let me in through the back door. The adult elephants were quite ferocious, spraying me with mucus from their trunks. The young man said they wouldn't allow even the feeders to approach them. The two-year-old calf was adorable, with endearing little wrinkles. Of course it didn't call me uncle because it couldn't speak any human language. But it was much friendlier than the adults. The young zookeeper used apples as bait to make it perform acts like shaking a bell, or playing with a basketball. It performed brilliantly. Its name was Erna.

Erna weighed 89 kg at birth and, not unlike a bovine calf, could rise to its feet minutes post-partum. An elephant cow in heat is irritable. It is not uncommon for her to spray people with water, hit them with her trunk or refuse to obey instructions, or even charge at people for no apparent reason. Mating does not take long, usually less than five minutes. There are two to three attempts at mating a day, with low odds of insemination. It takes seven months to confirm a pregnancy. When that happens, the teats of the elephant cow enlarge, as well as the belly. An adult bull eats ten times a day and consumes a total of about five hundred pounds of food, which includes broad-leaf grass, dried couch grass, rice, cereals, corn, bran, flour, apples, bananas, sugarcane, watermelons, carrots, kohlrabi, pumpkins, winter melon, bamboo leaves, moso bamboo shoots, straw, salt, bone meal and vitamins. The diet is vegetarian.

A bull sleeps for four hours a day, a cow for six hours and a calf for ten hours. The elephants dislike cold temperatures. Calves younger than a year are frightened by thunder.

Going into labor is painful for a pregnant elephant; it's not uncommon for a cow in labor to thrash about and cry in pain on the ground. When delivering, the pregnant cow parts her hind legs and raises her rump. The delivery time for a first pregnancy is about six hours and drops off precipitously to twenty minutes for a second pregnancy. The calf is born wrapped in the afterbirth, which will be torn open by the cow with her trunk. Normally one calf is birthed at a time, and a cow gives birth about once every five years. He said the skin of the young elephant was very smooth and fine and urged me to feel it. It felt rather rough to me. Erna had beautiful eyes, and they seemed to interact with humans. He said an elephant was worth about twenty thousand yuan. Mentally adding up all the elephants in China, I estimated the total worth would not exceed ten million yuan.

Did China have five hundred elephants?

It was an overcast day. I woke up feeling listless. I sat behind my desk looking out the window at the cement jungle, rows upon rows of tall buildings, their hundreds of windows staring back at me like so many eyes. It was frightening. There was not a spot of green to be found. Under the tyranny of hundreds of eyes I turned my thoughts to the Elephant.

It was a long time since last I gave it any thought. For a month now I had been kept busy by the New Year's holidays and idle chitchats with Lin Yi. If she did not stay at my place, she would call late in the night to make conversation since she couldn't fall asleep much as she tried. Her voice was affectionate and heartwarming, and the insomniac sleepiness in it was enough to produce a similar insomnia in me. I told her not to call again. If she needed to talk, why not come in person? That way we could talk while doing other interesting stuff. She said she was Lin Lin, not Lin Yi. There was no such person as Lin Yi. Are you a ghost, I asked. Are both of you ghosts?

"Yes."

A rustling sound could be heard at the other end, as if a ghost were creeping toward me along the phone line. I waited.

Nothing materialized.

To avenge my insomnia, I used my overflowing imagination to compose stories. I dashed off four in one breath: *Dad, A Family of Three, The Color Blue* and *The Old House*. My favorite was *The Color Blue*, because it gave an impression that it was not the work of a male writer. I put the Elephant aside for a while. I didn't want my recent unhealthy mood to rub off on him, corrupting him. He was still too young and too impressionable, and he was such an avid imitator.

Outside the window a spring rain was falling, accompanied by thunderclaps. When as a child I came upon Tang poet Du Fu's line "Good rain knows its time, When life grows in spring," I found it poorly written. When I grew older, I understood that the seemingly clumsy sentence "When life grows in spring" was not a feat attainable by just any old would-be poet. With age I have learned that water is of primary importance for humans and all other animals. Man has always chosen to live close to sources of water, as has my Elephant. With the arrival of the rainy season, the elephant herd was drenched and close to developing eczema. The thunderclaps made the younger elephants shake with fear. The moon, their protector, was obscured by thick dark clouds and all surrounding them was a gray expanse. In rain the wilderness sprang back to life, as grasses and trees grew furiously, to provide the proboscidians with food.

The rivers overflowed their banks, their usual channels now hidden under water. The hippos scurried about in excitement and the crocodiles lay in wait for carcasses. Hartebeests, gnus, zebras and rhinos trudged laboriously through the water. Rain had washed away the scents of the animals and the carnivorous predators' sense of smell became dulled. Mist and rain hovered above the flooded plains; in the distance big tree trunks and giraffes could be seen adrift in the water.

My Elephant, one among many refugees, raised his eyes skyward despite his mother's exhortation to look down at the rising water. He wondered why the proud sun had removed himself from the sky. Now the sky was as poor and desolate as the earth; there was nothing interesting to see. Up above and down below, there was a uniform drabness and muddiness.

The sound of thunder rang out.

The Elephant trailed his mother, who followed the herd toward higher ground. He held his trunk high to avoid choking on water. His mother gave him an occasional tug with her trunk. The rushing water made staying steady on one's feet difficult. He was repulsed by the water, and the joy he used to feel when playing with water had now completely disappeared. He was almost too tired to move and wanted to beg his mother to pause for a rest, but his mother kept on with her head held high. He rubbed his mother's teats with his trunk but his mother did not show any inclination to slow down to allow him to suckle. Sulking, the Elephant refused to continue the march. He was fed up with the ceaseless walking and the endless rain.

The herd widened its distance from the Elephant.

The Elephant was gripped by fear. His screaming fell on deaf ears. He scurried ahead on his short legs. He tripped and was borne away by the flood.

After half an hour in the bathroom I returned to my desk to continue the story about the Elephant, my mind partly distracted by the fear that sudden ringing of the telephone would disrupt my train of thought and kill my inspiration. The phone often rang when you least expected it.

It remained silent.

The thunderclaps continued. With the light turned off, the room was lit only by flashes of sickly white accompanying the assault of lightning and thunder. I was concerned about the fate of my Elephant. He had no roof to shelter him from the rain. During the rainy season countless numbers of animals drown on the African savannas, including my beloved elephants.

Lin Yi walked into the room in a peal of thunder. I did not hear the door open. She stood by my bed, dripping water everywhere. The skirt she wore was illuminated by the lightning.

"Are you afraid?"

I nodded.

Her voice trembled. I helped her out of her wet clothes and threw them on the floor. She picked them up and placed them on the desk. Why don't you fold them in a neat pile for good measure? Silly girl. I told her to get under the blanket and warmed her with my body. Her knees felt very cold.

"I thought I could wear a skirt whenever

it thundered." She kept her rigid body snug against mine. "My skirt is very pretty. Why don't you turn on the electric blanket? It won't give me an electric shock, will it? Two hooligans were chasing me because I was so pretty in my dress. I suppose I would chase me too if I were a hooligan."

"Shut your mouth, little one."

"What's the rush? You aren't a hooligan, so there's no hurry. I am staying for the night."

"There's not much night left. It will be light shortly."

"I'm staying for good. I will never leave again. I want you to warm me like this forever. You are so warm, so damn warm."

"Hey, watch your language. No curse words if you want to stay. You don't need to come to me. Just buy yourself an electric blanket. It's a whole lot damn warmer."

Lightning struck and thunder bellowed.

She shushed me with a frown, saying she almost forgot. Lying on her stomach she picked up the phone and dialed a number.

"Whose life are you messing up now?"

"I'm here. I'm fine. I'm all right."

"Whose life are you messing up now?"

She hung up, explaining it was Lin Lin on the phone.

I was by now totally confused. "Dial the number again. I want to speak to her."

"Lin Lin has no desire to speak to you."

"I want to speak to her, do you hear?"

"I am Lin Lin. Why can't you get it into your head? Lin Lin is me." She pulled the cover aside, "Look at me. Don't you remember this mole by my navel? You so enjoyed kissing it in that thatched hut."

Oh boy, did I remember it!

I pulled the cover over her.

"Don't be mad. You did not lose your temper like this in the past." She held my hand. "Your hand used to reach around the small of my back and rest on my shoulder. You enjoyed doing it like this, and this, and this. When I hugged you tightly you would push me away. You would hold me and then let go of me. You were mean when you told me to stop it. When you kissed me you always flattened my nose."

As if hypnotized, I let her take me into the past, following her instructions. And I was led to believe that that was what had happened in the past, when I was much younger.

"That day you said you couldn't do it. You said you had to finish what you started. I said I would wait for you. I said it was fine. Everything was fine as long as I was with you. We battled all night. And you said you began to feel like a man. That was how I wanted you to feel."

The sky was growing lighter.

"I am Lin Lin, and I am also Lin Yi. We are both yours. I always go back to the past. My elder sister never mentions you. Lin Yi is Lin Lin. Don't separate us. Please don't split us up."

For hours after daybreak, we lay in bed, reluctant to get up. Lin Yi drifted in and out of sleep. She said she was dead tired. I found that mole, dark and eye-catching. She told me to leave her alone. In that thatched hut, I tried to rouse her out of bed because the folks would arrive shortly. She said let them come; they would leave in embarrassment as soon as they found out about us. When the door seemed on the point of coming off its hinges with all the pounding and shaking, she disappeared under the blanket and urged me to do the same. Hey stop smoking! I finished the last set of my physical exercise amidst the pounding on the door and, panting heavily, railed against those outside the door.

The timeline was extremely blurry.

She finally woke up and stuck her tongue out at me. I gave her a playful slap and told her to get up and fix me something to eat.

"What do you want to eat?"

"Rice porridge. You make great rice porridge. You'll find some very nice Kirby cucumbers in the wall cabinet."

"I've never made porridge before. That was always the job of mother and Lin Lin. Lin Lin is excellent at making rice porridge."

"Lin Yi, call Lin Lin. I want to speak to her." I put the phone on her body, grabbed her hand and pulled out the index finger. "Say the number. I'll dial it."

"Stop bothering me." She jerked her hand free and moved the phone away from her, sitting up and exposing her striking mole. "I'll go make rice congee. Once, you ate four bowls of it. You said you had enough to last a lifetime and you'd never be hungry again. But you are hungry again."

I watched as she stood naked on the bed, reaching for article after article of my clothing. She buttoned up my shirt and pulled it on over her head like a sweatshirt. In the thatched hut, after she had pulled on my shirt, she proceeded to put on my underpants, then took them off, complaining about the coarseness and stiffness of the fabric. The shirt fell over her legs. After admiring herself in the mirror for a few moments she rolled up her sleeves and made her way to the kitchen, singing and clumping along in my shoes.

She took off my underpants that she had put on just a moment ago. Then, singing, she got off the bed and looked for my shoes.

The phone rang. I grabbed the receiver and all I heard was a busy tone.

"Damn! I'm going to smash this phone!"

"Honey, let me smash it for you!'

After the meal I took Lin Yi to a movie. Coming out of the theater she suggested a walk through the park on our way home. She went up to a swing and got on. She asked me to push her; the swing swung sideways as I pushed. She sat on the swing, listening to my account of the troubles I'd had while writing the elephant story.

"Why don't you just quit writing it? Then there will be no more troubles."

She often hit the nail on the head. If writing the story troubled me so much, it was only rational that I should just quit. But once I thought to write it, not writing it would be even more troubling. I could often picture that ancient, dying elephant walking alone in the wilderness and I would have the deep sense of having let it down.

"Did your Elephant die in the flood?"

"No."

"Too bad. It would have been nice if he'd

died."

"It'd be nice if you died, Lin Yi," I sighed. "You have less worth than an elephant. You wouldn't even leave a pair of tusks."

"Didn't you know?" she said with a surprised look, "I died a long time ago. If I were alive, would I have come to you? It's true I didn't leave behind a pair of tusks. Tusks are precious."

"Stop your damn nonsense!"

"I'm not talking nonsense." She asked me to stop pushing the swing. Still sitting on the swing, she took my hands and placed them like a vice around her neck. "Now squeeze, squeeze hard, like then. You won't be able to strangle me to death. Try it and you will know."

As if hypnotized, I slowly tightened the grip about her neck. Her soft, flexible neck became rigid and the stiffness hurt my hands. I relaxed my grip.

She threw up uncontrollably.

"What's the matter with you? Why didn't you go all the way? I feel worse than dying. You are useless. You can't even strangle a dead person. You were more savage then, unlike the award-winning gigolo that you are today. I've attached myself to the wrong man, in two successive lives. You make me sick. I don't even want to waste any tears on you. And you tried to show off your prowess, to act like a purebred gigolo! You are so pink and tender! And so damn sentimental …"

"Shut up! I fucked you."

SIX

The story was set aside for months, during which I was busy with one thing or another, or with nothing in particular. After a few inquiries, I finally found out something about the missing Elephant's whereabouts. The rainy season was now said to be over and I decided to continue to write about him.

I finished writing the last few words in Chapter 5 and came to the realization that a plot worthy of its name was shaping up for the story. That was not what had really happened that day. No matter how hard I pushed, Lin Yi couldn't get her swing to go into motion and she complained of lightheadedness. So she gave up. She gave me a kiss before getting off the swing and we headed home in silence.

When I showed the "plot" to Lin Yi, a sudden change came over her face and she unaccountably started to vomit, uncontrollably, as in the plot.

She said: "You have an X-ray eye."

She wanted me to keep it in, saying that was indeed what happened.

As I searched for my beloved Elephant, Lin Yi would pop in from time to time to ask about progress. If no new information was available, she would become dejected and rebuff my efforts at cheering her up. I couldn't figure out this change in her. She had always had an aversion to elephants. Now there was new information about the Elephant, though I hadn't verified it with my own eyes. The tip of the Elephant's trunk had not yet moistened my palm. Encouraged by the news, I decided to continue my account of his life. Lin Yi agreed with my decision and promised not to visit me for a week, so that the Elephant and I could have a proper reunion and talk about how much we missed each other.

I told her the Elephant actually didn't drift very far. After tumbling a few times in the flood and a few mouthfuls of water down his windpipe, he escaped with only a scratch. A clump of trees caught and saved him. He stumbled to higher ground and surveyed the forlorn environment for a glimpse of his mother. There was not a trace of her.

He walked into the jungle.

Then his slight frame disappeared into the dense trees. Somehow he survived. When he reemerged, his size had doubled, although he was dirty and appeared exhausted.

The flood had receded. The wilderness now teemed with animals, as if there had never been a flood.

The Elephant was looking for his herd. He missed the warmth of group life and his mother's teats. No other animal dared to stand in his way. This foreshadowed his future roaming. On the one hand he felt an overwhelming loneliness; on the other, a vague attraction to solitude. Other than the birds that occasionally alighted on his back for brief rests, no other animal was foolhardy enough to venture near him. Elephants have always stayed exclusively with their own kind.

In solitude he learned to talk to himself.

Where had the oceans of water gone? Even the huge trees had been uprooted; water was greater than even elephants. Now, it too was gone, traveling on alien territory, just like me. Did it miss its mother's breasts?

Why did the moon disappear when water appeared?

He looked at his reflection in a waterhole and wallowed in it all afternoon. Deer and lions stood nearby in separate groups, afraid to disturb his pleasant dreaming. He rolled in the hole, covering his body with the cool, fine mud. Drawing water through his trunk, he sprayed the lions, who backed away. More animals were gathering around the waterhole, like spectators around a bullring. The Elephant couldn't help feeling a little proud. He even relished the hostility in the eyes of the carnivores.

Dusk fell.

When dusk fell, a gradual changing of colors ensued, first to yellow, then red, until everything turned gray and eventually faded into darkness. Then the moon would rise.

The Elephant lay down and fell asleep.

While I had been quarrelling with Lin Yi, the Elephant had grown with surprising speed. I asked Lin Yi what had happened. She told me not to interfere, no matter what the Elephant did. She resented man's interference with nature. She said humans should pay more attention to human affairs.

"There's no more nature left, Lin Yi. Maybe there's still some left in the desert. The desert is the last sanctuary of nature, being uninhabited by man. Man is the most unnatural of beings and he is even taking nature away from nature. Even my Elephant could not enjoy nature undisturbed. But I try hard to protect him from the corruption of the human world. The Elephant has not yet been exposed to any biped called man; nor has he ever been spotted by one. He lives in an imaginary space; it's only there that he can breathe freely. I have to remain vigilant."

"He has been seen by you," Lin Yi said, "Your reconnoitering eyes have relentlessly tracked him. He owes his birth to you. Without you keeping an eye out for him, he loses all meaning."

"He doesn't owe it to me."

"Why?"

"There's no such thing as owing life to me. Life begins by itself, and ends by itself."

"His life is dependent on you. You influenced his birth."

"Don't be silly, Lin Yi. It is he that has influenced me. Because of him, you and I couldn't even make love without getting distracted. Don't you think? He is much stronger than I."

We were talking in the kitchen. Lin Yi said she was an expert when it came to cooking noodles. I admitted my weakness in that department and watched her do it. I leaned against the sink watching her cook the noodles into a paste-like mush. Then I told her that despite my humble origin I never ate mush.

"Just make do this once. You'll like it so much you won't want to put it down. I saw some fermented bean curd. It goes perfectly with the mush."

"No."

"Don't lie. When we were down in the boondocks you ate it with gusto when it was still piping hot and your mouth scalded. You said you had been converted to the cult of the mush."

"Did that really happen?"

"When we kissed, you said it hurt."

I still couldn't recall it. Why should I always be forced to remember what she said had happened?

Nearly in despair, Lin Yi suddenly remembered a detail that put all my denials to rest.

"It happened on your birthday."

SEVEN

All details involving Lin Lin lay at Lin Yi's fingertips. I couldn't remember all that she remembered about Lin Lin, but eventually I admitted to everything. I suspect she accomplished this by suggestion. Lin Yi was an expert of suggestion. And I was particularly susceptible to suggestion.

I mentioned several times to Lin Yi my interest in visiting her home, which was quite far and which I had visited regularly years ago. Lin Yi said she'd moved even farther away.

"What if I don't mind the distance?"

"No. I mind even if you don't."

I begged her for one little visit. I had traveled frequently to faraway Africa to visit my Elephant. I was not afraid of walking the great distance even though I didn't possess a pair of strong, muscular legs. I said we could take a taxi.

"Then you go by yourself."

"Give me the address of your home."

"I have a home but it has no address."

"Stop being ridiculous."

Lin Yi finally agreed to go with me.

I did not hire a taxi. It was too expensive. A friend of mine who drove a Daihatsu was willing to help. His name was Wang Zongfu, a happy young man, who had always dreamed of one day trading in his Daihatsu for a Nissan or a Mercedes. He drove taxis for eight years and was familiar with the highways and back alleyways of Shanghai.

Wang Zongfu was a smoker and he smoked when he drove but otherwise observed the traffic regulations. Since it would be bad form to speak exclusively to Lin Yi in the car, I told him about my elephant story. He ribbed me for having nothing better to do. With so many human stories waiting to be written, why would anyone write about an elephant? I told him not to belittle the elephants. With a shake of its head, an elephant could upend the Daihatsu he was driving. The tusks would go in this side of the vehicle and come out the other side of it, and the people inside would be nailed to their seats like pinned butterfly specimens. Xiao Wang dismissed it as hot air.

"It isn't hot air, brother. The elephant skin alone weighs a ton, the two ears weigh eighty kilos, the trunk weighs one hundred and twenty kilos and the tusks one hundred and nine kilos."

"I don't stand a chance then," he said.

As he drove, Xiao Wang frequently eyed Lin Yi in the rearview mirror. I asked them if they knew each other, they said they didn't. Xiao Wang was more tactful in saying he vaguely remembered having seen her somewhere. I introduced her as my girlfriend, saying she was Lin Yi and her elder sister Lin Lin had been my girlfriend in the past.

"Wasn't Heipi your former girlfriend?" Wang Zongfu asked innocently.

"Heipi left me."

It was a subject I would rather not dwell on. It was perhaps with ulterior motives that Xiao Wang asked slyly about my daughter Tian Tian and how she was doing. He asked about her hair, her teeth and how far along she was in learning to walk. After rattling off his questions, he glanced in the rearview mirror.

I told him that my daughter Tian Tian was healthy, and I gave an account of the growth of her hair and teeth and what not. I said that since I was writing a novel, there was neither daughter nor wife and I was living alone in an old house, eating irregularly, missing meals. If I had not been writing a novel, there wouldn't have been a Lin Yi. Lin Yi, like my Elephant, owed their existence to the writing of this story.

Wang Zongfu said, chuckling, I just can't figure out people like you.

Lin Yi said, also with a laugh, she was no longer feeling drowsy. She asked me for a cigarette, pinched off the filter tip, lit it, and started blowing smoke-rings. The rings escaped from her pursed lips, floating and swirling toward the front to envelope Xiao Wang's head before dissolving as they hit the windshield. We stopped to rest midway and had some soft drinks. When we returned to the car, Lin Yi got into the front passenger seat to give directions to Xiao Wang. The sky was overcast; it had been like that for over a fortnight now. After making many turns in the labyrinthine network of alleys, the Daihatsu entered a vacant lot. Xiao Wang said the houses originally sitting here must have been torn down for a new railroad station, or a water diversion project in the upper reaches of the Huangpu River. Or it was the work site of the Yan'an East Road tunnel under the river. The car tires got mired in the mud several times and there was a real danger of getting completely stuck. It was an unlucky afternoon, we had to change a tire once. With great patience Wang Zongfu drove in circles, looking for the place. Lin Yi finally declared she was confused and had lost her bearings.

We all got out of the car.

I found in the rubble a pink plastic toy elephant, just like mine. Lin Yi found a few buttons and a hair pin. She pointed to a stone that looked like a stepping stone used for mounting a horse and said this must be the place. She had stayed the night here only two days before and had agreed with Lin Lin that the window pane must be replaced the following week. How come it had been razed to the ground and reduced to a pile of rubble in such a short time?

Lin Yi started to cry.

I was unable to calm her down. Xiao Wang told a joke and through her tears she broke into a smile.

I didn't laugh because I had heard the joke so many times. Xiao Wang's repertory of jokes was exclusively about tormented husbands. They lost the ability to elicit laughter after too many repetitions. But he did have some good ones that were actually quite funny.

Once back at my house Lin Yi couldn't wait to

make a phone call. The call went through.

"Lin Lin, I couldn't find you today."

Lin Yi, with her back to me, was careful not to give me a chance to grab the phone from her. I walked over to her and placed a hand on the top of her head; she shuddered.

After a long while, she handed the receiver to me and all I heard was static, followed by a busy signal.

"Lin Lin said that we were unable to find her because you came along. She said she didn't want to see you."

I put the phone back into its cradle and told her I knew.

That night we shared one bottle of beer and skipped supper. After she went to bed, Lin Yi tossed and turned in a fitful sleep. It interfered with my writing of the elephant story.

"Sleep well, Lin Yi. Sweet dreams."

"It's no good. I can't sleep well when I think that I have no home to go back to. What am I without a home? I don't want to beg you to let me stay. I'll leave tomorrow and never come back again."

It didn't make a difference to me whether Lin Yi had a home or not. Since she was here, she might as well stay. We didn't have to beg each other for anything. I told her not to make a big deal out of nothing. I said I was not in the mood for flirting at the moment. I ignored her and plunged back into my story, continuing to track my Elephant. He had widened the distance between us. With my bad legs, it would be hard for me to catch up if he went too far ahead.

The Elephant watched me from a great distance, gave a few flourishes of his trunk and moved on, flapping his ears.

I realized that many years had gone by and he was now powerfully built and fine-featured. At one time I held his trunk and gave him an account of my life. He was really tickled. Giving my shoulder a few pats with his trunk he said I had had a strange life. When I mentioned the entry about elephants in the *Concise Encyclopedia Britannica*, he told me not to believe all that nonsense. An elephant is an elephant. Cut out the fancy stuff.

I asked the Elephant if he had ever dated. He said not yet. He believed falling in love was silly. I recounted some folk stories from the human world, such as the Cowherd and the Girl Weaver, Liang Shanbo and Zhu Yingtai and Sister Lin and Brother Bao of the *Dream of the Red Chamber*. They only elicited endless yawns from him.

The Elephant had now hit puberty and would inexplicably lose his temper, breaking tree trunks as a result. He was paying more attention to the reproductive behavior of other elephants. I became worried for him. But he was truly an elephant with class. He never utter profanities and was uninterested by lewd stories about elephants.

The female elephants circled about him at a distance while he continued to graze in peace and serenity. A female elephant of a certain age walked up to him and playfully ran her trunk across his back and rump. He walked away quietly, leaving the female elephant in a mild state of shock.

EIGHT

Over the past few months I have frequently picked up my half-finished manuscripts to reread them. It is shaping up to be a dud of a story. The Elephant has all along voiced strong objections to being written about; as have Lin Lin and Lin Yi, who do not look kindly on exposing their private relationships to public scrutiny.

I am in a dilemma.

One day my friend Wen Fei dropped by for a visit and flipped through my manuscripts. She had shaved her head, which glittered in the light. She said she was writing about shaved heads and so far had written three thousand words. Seeing how dejected I was, she suggested I take over and finish her story. I didn't take her up on the offer, fearing future copyright complications. Wen Fei, with her head shaved down to her bluish scalp, was indeed beautiful and somewhat alluring. Running my hand across the top of her head, I said if a monk could do this to you, surely I could too. She said please act your age, lewd old man! Maybe I had offended her; she now wanted to leave. When I offered the last bit of Coca Cola left in the house, she refused to drink it, saying she was going home to wait for a phone call. I copied a song about waiting to hear from a friend and handed it to her, saying she could sing it when she got bored while waiting.

I implored her to talk a bit about elephants.

She said some people were reincarnated from monkeys, others from snakes, fish or cicadas, and still others from elephants.

After Wen Fei left, I relayed our conversation to the Elephant, who mulled it over and said she was probably right.

In retrospect, another person who wouldn't leave me alone was Lin Yi. Twenty thousand words into the story and I was still unable to find a proper place for her in the story. Lin Yi demurred; she said the story was fine the way it was. She didn't care about having a proper place. She couldn't care less.

But I had a nagging feeling that the process of creating Lin Yi was flawed. Once a flaw crept into the creative process, writing further became seriously arduous. Seeing my frustration, Lin Yi lay down beside me and whispered softly: don't be too hard on yourself. The radio was playing an arrangement of the Bach/Gounod Ave Maria, a chaste song that even chaste girls had difficulty mastering.

"Change the story as you wish. I defer to your wisdom."

"Since when have you deferred to me?"

"I'm pregnant." She took my hand and placed it on her vast, flat abdomen. "I already knew I was pregnant the day we went looking for my home."

"Is it my child?"

"It is yours."

I immediately decided that we hadn't gone looking for that vanishing house that day. That would terminate her pregnancy. I also decided that we had never indulged in that pleasurable, solemn exercise. Yes, we kissed, hugged, caressed, but we never had intercourse. We didn't simultaneously reach that altitude. I proposed that Lin Yi's virginity be restored and that carnal desire be capped at an appropriate level. I was willing to start with a clean slate, again and again.

"Of course I am still a virgin," Lin Yi said, putting on her clothes and stepping off the bed. She was touchingly chaste. I studied her face.

"I already feel much lighter now that I no longer need to be pregnant. Suffering should end with this generation. You've made up so many lewd episodes about Lin Lin and me luring you into repeated sessions of physical exercise because you knew there had never been any. You made everything up to achieve your own psychological balance. You understood that without Lin Lin there wouldn't have been me. If I were Lin Lin, I would be repaying you for your super-human love. If I were Lin Yi, then I would be bent on revenge."

"I understand. I am waiting."

"I can't sleep in peace when I think that I will kill you sooner or later.

"I'll save you the trouble. I'll die by my own hand."

Chaste tenderness gave way to hostility in Lin Yi's face. My volunteering to die by my own hand agitated her.

"Are you trying to ruin me? If I don't get to kill you, I'd have come in vain. No, I will not tolerate your suicide. I am not killing you for the thrill of the readers. I don't need any readers. If I were Lin Lin, killing you would constitute repayment of a kindness. If I were Lin Yi, killing you would be repaying a kindness on behalf of Lin Lin. You must save yourself for me. Your life belongs to us. You created us and by the same token we created you."

"The act of creation saps your strength. Even God needed to rest after his exhausting creative work. Lin Yi, I'm already tired from merely thinking of the need for me to create a you to create me."

"More tiring than killing a person?" Lin Yi came back with a sharp retort. "More tiring than killing Lin Lin?"

"Yes."

"Is there anything more tiring than that?"

"There is. Waiting to be killed is more tiresome."

"I also am waiting."

I felt sorry for her, a girl burdened with such an onerous mission. I held out my hand and she took it. We both saw the ending. We had to be honest, then we'd feel relieved, and finally we'd be distraught.

"There may yet be a different ending," Lin Yi said, "It always happens with your novels. When the story of the Elephant began, you had eyes only for the Elephant and I was invisible to you. When I first came into the picture, there was no thought of killing or being killed. You became obsessed with me as soon as you saw me."

"Now that it's been thought of, there's bound

to be a killing." I said evenly. I was grateful for Lin Yi's good will but I didn't expect to be spared by a stroke of luck.

"You can always revise the parts about me. Only, don't make me into a clone of your old flames. You've created too many clones, girls that always talk the way I am talking at this very moment. They love you, protect you, always with a bit of melancholy. I want you to make me over. I have more gumption than your other girls. It is I who bear a grudge and these hands of mine that are holding yours will one day commit an inhumane act. These days I have come to the conclusion that in previous life I was probably an elephant. I'm happy to be an elephant, living only in the jungle, just like your Elephant. Yes, that's how I want you to make me over."

"Let me think about it."

"Then let's go to sleep."

Before turning off the light Lin Yi kissed me. She then glared at me, her eyes filled with hostility. I turned off the light and lay down on the makeshift bed—a mat—on the floor by her bed. I couldn't see what she was doing.

It took a long time for me to fall asleep—perhaps because I was not accustomed to it?

In the middle of the night I was woken by a phone call. She asked me to take good care of Lin Yi, to cherish her. It was a soft and serene voice. I thought that must have been Lin Lin.

I could no longer go back to sleep after the phone call, so I smoked a few cigarettes, thinking about Lin Lin. I couldn't be certain whether Lin Lin had also been a figment of my imagination. But I remembered there were several versions of how it ended for her.

I sat on the edge of the bed and placed my hand on Lin Yi's forehead. She was in a deep, peaceful sleep, just as Lin Lin used to be. In one ending for Lin Lin there was a night like this, with the lights dimmed. It was a dark night, dark as the moment just before the Elephant's coming into being. I caressed her hands. I loved Lin Yi; I loved this pair of hands that were destined to extinguish my life. She had

thin, puny hands. I wish I could trade hands
with her. My hands were stronger and more
experienced.

All of a sudden I realized Lin Yi's wrathful
eyes were glaring at me.
From that day on I worked doubly hard so that
I could finish this novel before the moment of
truth arrived. Lin Yi grew silent and took to
wearing white tops and black skirts, moving
about like a phantom. I found a copy of *Strange
Tales from a Chinese Studio* and handed it to
her. She took it, without flinching, and started
reading it sitting on the edge of the bed, that
is, behind me. "These tales are real," she said.
I ignored her and embarked on my African
safari. I turned my head after having traveled
some distance and Lin Yi had disappeared
without a trace.

When I met the Elephant, I couldn't resist
the urge to recount to him the story about *The
Legend of White Snake.* The Elephant asked
me if the story had any truth to it. When he
learned that it was just a story, he immediately
lost all interest. He wanted to hear me tell real

stories, the story of mankind.

So I started from how man had discovered fire and went on to the story of "Star Wars."

The Elephant listened quietly and gave a loud snort whenever the story really excited him. In the long storytelling session, there were a few times where he shed tears and once choking with sobs, wiped at his eyes with his trunk when I mentioned how the cattle industry came into being. After crying for a long time, he stoically asked me to go on.

"Why is history monopolized by man?" the Elephant asked earnestly.

I told the Elephant that I felt ashamed for man.

"Feeling ashamed. That's all you humans are good at."

I felt ashamed for man's being only good at feeling ashamed.

The grueling round of human history caused the Elephant to lose some pounds.

Every day the Elephant woke up before I did. Taking into account the difference between time zones, it would be me who watched the Elephant awake. The sun passes over my head before moving toward Africa. The blazing sun of an African high noon can scorch the thick skin of the elephants.

The elephants threw sand on their backs.

My Elephant lived among the others in the herd. His mother had birthed another calf. The herd, having slipped away from humans, now lived an anonymous life, out of the limelight, in an endless cycle of foraging, travel, play, reproduction and raising their young.

And, of course, death.

The Elephant had witnessed the death of an adolescent male member of the herd. A decayed tree trunk had fallen on the helpless young bull, crushing it to death. Other elephants had worked together to move the dead tree off the victim and had helped him to his feet with their trunks, but as soon as they had let go, he had toppled onto the grass, moaning with pain. The elephants stood in a circle around him until he died. Then they hauled some twigs to cover up the body. A mound was built in the jungle. The elephants kept vigil at the mound for a couple of days before leaving.

The moon hung high in the sky.

Is this what death is? The Elephant asked himself.

So, there is this thing called "death" that awaits him. It's so easy to die. Every elephant has to die once. Death means callous abandonment. Death is this mound. I also know how to build a mound like this.   .

In dejection the Elephant sprawled out on the ground, having lost the desire to go on. The female elephant that had protected him just he was born nudged him with her trunk, first with gently and then with greater force. But he was reluctant to continue the march. Since he would meet with death no matter where he went, he might as well stay put, like a mountain, or a mound. At least he would be still alive when he could hear the lament and sobbing of other elephants mourning him.

The herd walked away in silence. There was only the sound of branches and twigs snapping. The dour-faced baboons looked on in anger.

The female elephant, his protector, came closer to him. "Get up, my child, my man, you must stand up. No elephant has died this way. Although all elephants die, some deaths are weightier than Kilimanjaro and others lighter than a blade of grass."

The Elephant flapped his ears, still not budging.

The female elephant lowered herself to his height, and lightly rubbed his body, again and again. The Elephant accepted the massage quietly, increasingly conscious of the smooth beauty of his skin. He reciprocated the rubbing. The Elephant stood up.

"There's no hurry, my man," the female elephant said softly. She stood waiting patiently, knowing he would get it right. She wanted to savor this height of ecstasy.

(Three thousand words expunged here,) the Elephant dismounted calmly. He felt strong, fulfilled, unbelievably blissful. He gently tapped the shoulder of the cow and pulled her toward him.

Death is impossible, he thought.

NINE

Even as the plot thickens, Lin Yi remains an enigma. Whether in the early lovey-dovey role or as the later chaste maiden plotting revenge, Lin Yi has been elusive and ambiguous. The story has come to a point where I've lost control over its development. It has taken on a life of its own, and I don't know where it will end.

I would gladly see the story of the Elephant reduced to its original simplicity; a simple story is often the best story. At one time I pushed myself to write detective stories, with a view to practicing narrative sequence. If this were a crime story, the essential plot would had been laid bare and the end set in stone. But there is a difference. It may very well be that at the end no killer will be found and no stolen jewelry will be returned. The two breathtakingly beautiful tusks will remain firmly lodged in the elephant's gum, as hard to remove as it would be to try pulling out an incisor from a live tiger. This could turn out to be a good story that disappoints.

But I'm still going to continue writing, as it's the most outstanding story since the invention of the story genre. I'll try my best to tell the story in a grating voice. I've always dashed off my novels in a hurry; I will make an exception for this story. Haste gets in the way of good storytelling.

To finish this story is not only intended as a form of giving thanks to Acheng for the gift of his book but also meant to enable me to finally send back the other three books, which Hong Zi had loaned to me. These books were public property and it would be inappropriate to keep them for long. Moreover, I have sought a peace of mind by writing the story. I wanted to write about Lin Lin, who, truth be told, is the heart of this novel.

I know better than anyone that I will not get to see her again for the rest of my life. After the completion of the novel, I am going to give her a copy of the manuscripts via Lin Yi. I'm sure Lin Yi will agree to do it. She knows about everything that happened between Lin Lin and me. She knows how much I miss her.

Lin Yi appears and disappears without warning. Every time I stick my key in the door of my apartment I immediately would feel anxious, both fearing and craving her presence. She could spend a whole day reading *Strange Tales from a Chinese Studio* or some other novel, without uttering a single word to me. She left piles of novels by Agatha Christie and others on my desk, with slips of paper scribbled with undecipherable marks sandwiched between pages.

"You have read all of these books?" I asked nonchalantly.

"Yes, every word of them."

I told Lin Yi that I only liked *The Day of*

the Jackal. The movie was a bomb but the book was good. The Jackal had elevated killing to an art. The book left all other books of the genre in the dust.

"That's because you men live in a dream."

What male author, she said, could match Agatha Christie? She was a master of plotting and wrote in measured prose. Under her pen, there was romance even in murder. She was a genius. As she reeled off the virtues of Christie, Lin Yi's eyes glittered as if in rapture.

Lin Yi was uncharacteristically concerned about the fate of the Elephant; she urged me not to wreak havoc on the Elephant's life. She bought bunches of bananas that she wanted me to give to her proboscidean brother. I carried out her instructions. I avoided the subject of Lin Lin when I was with her.

Every time I returned from Africa, I would find my room occupied by Lin Yi. I would hear her singing, until I stuck my key into the keyhole. But on that occasion, after I had delivered the bananas, there was no singing, which disappointed me a little. But then I thought that was just as well; I was exhausted and the only thought I had was to get a good sleep.

I went into the kitchen to pour myself a glass of water. It tasted normal; I was confident Lin Yi wouldn't have poisoned the water. After washing the mud off my feet, I dropped onto the plank bed but immediately jumped up in shock.

I could almost see Lin Lin.

She sat on a corner of the bed, with her legs crossed. Under the light coming in from a streetlight, a pale smile played on her face. She was wearing the same clothes she'd worn back when we were together. They were old but clean.

I nearly fainted.

I cocked my ears to listen closely and heard something; she was singing:

A girl without a mother
Should be shunned by all.
A girl who's lost her mother
Will not leave you alone.

I lay down, resting my head on Lin Lin's leg, closing my eyes and my mouth. My heart beat wildly, as I awaited her announcement. This was the night when all stories would break.

I rested my head on Lin Yi. She tousled my hair with her hand, then pushed me to one side. I lay there, with my head resting on my arm, my eyes and mouth shut, waiting for her announcement.

She hummed the tune over and over again.

Late, very late into the night, Lin Yi said:

"Today is Lin Lin's birthday. It is also my birthday."

That night I didn't sleep on the floor. I lay fully clothed, lethargic, unwilling to move a muscle. Lin Yi took off Lin Lin's old clothes and changed into her pajamas. With my back next to hers, I couldn't go to sleep. I could feel her trembling.

She turned around, her quivering hands reaching out to me.

I took her into my arms. Her entire body shook uncontrollably. I could almost hear the tears fall. Her mission made her face a tough choice.

"Don't, Lin Yi. Wait until you are ready, when you can do a clean job. Wait a little longer. I'll always be at your disposal."

"No!"

She continued to unbutton my clothes.

"Think about the Elephant! The elephant that ate your bananas, your brother. My death will have repercussions for him. Wait some more, if only for the Elephant."

Lin Yi let me go, crying inconsolably as she put on her pajamas. She cried until it was almost light, when she finally fell asleep.

It was a sleepless night for me. I spent the night rummaging through my memory for Lin Lin's ending.

After hearing the story of mankind, the Elephant seemed to lose his appetite. He only picked at fruits, which had always been one of his favorites. I told him not to try to lose weight like the humans. Weight loss was a trivial pursuit invented by people who had gone on a binge. The Elephant, shaking his head, said that was not the reason; he had simply temporarily lost his appetite. I concluded that he must be suffering from anorexia nervosa, which killed the great singer Karen Carpenter. The Elephant said I shouldn't make such dire conclusions. Man was the natural enemy of elephants and elephants would not perish from the same disease that killed man.

"You said that elephants had once roamed what is today Henan Province of China. Where did those elephants go?"

"They died off. All of them."

"And we are the few that are left?"

"You could say that."

"What about the human population?"

"The human population has grown to five billion, with a daily addition of two hundred and twenty thousand more, which is many times the total population of elephants."

"Is that fair?"

"It isn't fair."

The Elephant was deeply frustrated. Compared to his frustration, human frustrations would appear affected and disingenuous.

"You are the most unfair animal on earth," the Elephant said, pointing at me with his trunk.

"I'm afraid so."

"Aren't you worried about the revenge of the elephants?"

"There's no way the elephants will be able to exact revenge on humans." I supplied some information about weaponry. "The greatest revenge of the elephants would be the self-inflicted, wholesale extinction of the entire family of Elephantidae. There is no other way for the elephants to punish man."

"What if I kill you?" the Elephant asked menacingly, "this very moment!"

"Two opposing armies will not kill each other's messengers," I added hastily, "I am only one in five billion. Killing me won't solve your problem. Man is much more prolific than you."

"Does man have no enemies of consequence then?"

"Yes, he does. Man is his own worst enemy.

They will soon grow to six billion, ten billion. Man is much crueler to man than to the elephants."

"Serves them right!" the Elephant said righteously.

In the quiet of night when even the Elephant was asleep, a few fragments of the past would drift into my mind. I could clearly and vividly see Lin Lin's elephant-shaped pencil sharpener. It was a green elephant without tusks. After Lin Lin's death I couldn't find it among her belongings.

In a milder version of my memory, Lin Lin did not pass away. My hands were still clean and I didn't need to wash them a dozen times every day. She was transferred back to Shanghai in a case of "hardship transfer." When the parents of a youth sent down to the countryside had no other children staying with them, the youth was allowed by policy to return to the parents in the city. After her hardship transfer back to Shanghai, I lost touch with her. When I was subsequently also transferred back to the city,

I didn't seek her out.

In yet another version of my memory, she stayed in the countryside and married a peasant. Rumor had it that she was beaten up by her husband when she asked him for permission to sit for a college entrance examination. Her resolve was further eroded by her son's sobbing and beseeching. With a sigh she gave up on the idea. If the rumor was true, then she must still be out there, working the fields. Or she may have become a specialized farmer breeding angora rabbits or medicinal ground beetles (Eupolyphaga sinensis), or running a small store, earning a living as a seamstress, making and selling bean curd, or tending to a small food stall. Since I left the village I had not kept up up to date with what was happening there, so I had no way of knowing for sure.

When I revisited the past, it was often with a heavy heart and knitted brows: I had let down so many people. Among the different versions of my recollections, I had a preference for the one with gore. It was a clean-cut story. In it Lin Lin died in the end. She lived only for the duration of her phone conversations with Lin Yi.

I confided all these thoughts to Lin Yi. She suggested that next time I had such nightmares I should pinch my leg. She told me that Lin Lin was doing well, and was living a perfectly happy life. "Don't disturb her. You already let her down once."

I nodded.

After a long while Lin Yi said: "Frankly, I wouldn't know whether she is happy or not."

Since Lin Yi reverted to being a virgin, I'd accompanied her to many performances. She didn't like chamber music, preferring instead concertos and opera. She said it was she who accompanied me to the performances. Really just two different ways of saying the same thing. In intermission she left the concert hall and didn't come back for the second half of the show. I sat accompanied by the bag on the vacant seat next to mine, until the theater emptied. She waited for me at the entrance of the theater.

"I had to take care of something."

"Okay."

"Where's my bag?"

"It's in my bag."

"Give it back to me. Now."

On our way home, she clutched her bag tightly, looking quite silly and awkward, as if she had an illegitimate child in her arms and she was torn between love and embarrassment. Her arms remained rigid even when we arrived at home.

"Relax. Your beloved baby is no longer in danger. You can put it down now."

Lin Yi put her bag down as if having come out of a trance. I asked if I could take a look and she said that was why she had brought the bag—to show me its contents.

In the bag were two diaries kept by Lin Lin, as well as one hundred and one letters I'd written to her.

"Where did you get it?"

"Lin Lin gave it to me."

Rereading my own letters, I realized how much I'd aged. I had been young then, like the

Elephant, and had probably felt just as invincible. In the first letter, I told a story about two people who had met under mysterious circumstances and parted under mysterious circumstances. I confidently predicted their reunion, but a reunion in which the two people, covered with rust, no longer recognized each other. It was as if I was trying to put a philosophical gloss on the letter, to sound mystical, different, or prophetic. From the second one on, they began to read more like letters. I wrote about the silly things that someone who sorely misses someone else is capable of. Sages, ancient and modern, as well as poets and leading lights of literature were cited. Eventually the quotations dwindled to a trickle until only my soliloquies were left.

Reading letters was like reading someone else's story. My penmanship is not what it used to be. The handwriting in the letters was rich in affection and emotion, and while lacking in ease and liberty and neatness, it was quite in character with a decent, as yet unsophisticated lad. Nowadays my handwriting goes every which way, untrammeled and unrestrained in an affected sort of way.

On the inside cover of Lin Lin's diary was a photograph of her, a dead ringer of today's Lin Yi. I ran my fingers across the photo, caressing her eyes and her hair. She looked serenely at me.

"Are you okay?"

"Don't be silly."

Lin Yi closed the diary.

I looked at Lin Yi as I ran my hand over her hair and her eyes. Her eyes remained open, full of cold indifference. My hand instantly froze and was withdrawn.

TEN

Nighttime in the jungle was not peaceful. It was a darkness that bordered on blue. Sounds of carnivores on the prowl could be heard far and near. Had it not been for the company of the Elephant, I would have been terrified. The Elephant performed a flourish with his trunk, showing scorn for the nervous wreck that I was reduced to.

We ate bananas while chitchatting.

When I broached the subject of death, the Elephant flapped his ears, signaling that it was all water under the bridge now. He felt he was bursting with life and claimed he could rebuild the nation of elephants, eager for compliments about his reproductive prowess. But I did not give him that satisfaction. He had had no past accomplishments in this regard to bolster his claim, his experience being limited to that one time with that middle-aged cow. That single experience was enough to kindle his nation-building zeal.

He asked me why Lin Yi was not with me. I said we were having a conversation between men, why would we want a woman here? He said he couldn't tell a human male from a female. I told him he could tell by looking to see if there was hair around the mouth. He said you called that hair? It was barely visible. I said alternatively he could look at the tongue. Women usually wagged their tongues a lot more than men. He said all humans wagged their tongues too much, if you asked him. They had nothing better to do.

After finishing the bananas, the Elephant said to me that he had an urgent task. He was going to search for his roots.

"Do elephants have roots too?"

"Why not?"

He said he was going to find his father.

The Elephant started his search that very night. Snuggling up to his mother, he beseeched her to try to remember who his father was. In the fog of sleep his mother tried to discourage his importunate demands. "For elephants fathers don't count. All adult bulls are your fathers. Male elephants have no place in the elephant lineage." He fell silent, saddened that he was also a male and therefore had no place in the pedigree, and his children would not know who their father was.

I tried to console him, saying the identity of the father was really not that important. In fury he hoisted me high in the air with his trunk and threatened to make a projectile of me if I dared interject another wise word. Elephants could take care of their own affairs; humans should stay out of it. Humans knew who their father was; even illegitimate children had a father.

He deposited me on his back and told me to get off on my own.

I decided to kibitz one more time: if the

male elephants were willing to cooperate, I was ready to conduct a blood test on them, which would identify his father. It was a method used also by humans to trace parentage.

"Elephants have no use for such roundabout methods," the Elephant said angrily and told me to get off his back at once.

You stupid elephant! What's the use of having such a damn big head! You'll never find your father. Your mother is a whore who has fooled around with so many she no longer remembers one from another.

I cursed mentally as I slid down off the Elephant's back, scraping my calf against the rough skin. The Elephant, his big, unwieldy head cocked to one side, watched me make a fool of myself.

"You are cursing me. I can smell it."

"Yes."

"I said all humans wagged their tongues; you take the prize. Elephants prefer physical fights. So throw down your gauntlet."

I immediately thought of Lin Yi. Maybe I should bid her a mental farewell. After all she had first claim on ending my life.

"Throw down the gauntlet. I won't hit you. I will let you hit me until you kill me or die from exhaustion. But I won't allow you to denigrate elephants. Hit me as hard as you like but no cursing, no matter how good you are at tongue-wagging. If you want to play with elephants, you play by their rules."

I had little doubt that I would end up dying of exhaustion that night. I refused to attack him; I'd much sooner kill myself by butting my head against one of his columnar legs. His leg was big enough for ten people to simultaneously dash their brains against it.

A huge silhouette flashed by in the jungle.

"If you are not ready to fight, you can go back, my friend. You are not a good sport. You pick on those weaker than you and are afraid to confront the strong ones. Come back when you're ready to fight."

With that, the Elephant broke into a trot to chase after that shadow.

After being thus humiliated by him, I was no longer in the mood to track the Elephant. I even stooped so low as to think of a gun.

A gun!

Ever since I knew him, I'd wanted very much to scratch the Elephant's trunk. But that was a no-no. As much as the Elephant was a generous and gentle soul, he would not tolerate the disrespect and contempt implied by someone scratching his trunk. Elephants have great pride, and I honor their self-respect.

I've devoted a great deal of time to the Elephant and have even modified my schedule to be in sync with his African time zone, at the expense of Lin Yi, I must admit. She strongly resented this reversal of night and day.

Late in the night, when the Elephant was grazing leisurely, I found myself unoccupied. The Elephant deployed his long trunk to pull up the clumps of grass, roots and all, and thrashed them against his forelegs to shake off the mud before throwing them into his mouth. The movement was as neat and fluid as the dunking action of an American professional basketball player. The Elephant, elegant in demeanor, never ate tree bark. I could watch him do it for hours on end. While watching the Elephant I remained aware of the stirrings of Lin Yi lying by my side. She gritted her teeth while sleeping. Her beautiful, long, slender neck rested next to one of my hands. I gripped the hand with my other hand.

Since that day, Lin Yi no longer allowed me to sleep on the floor. She wanted me to sleep next to her, face to face. She went to great lengths to tempt me, seducing me with her eyes and her body, slowly breaking down my resistance by playing on my compassion. Lin Yi even tried angering me into ravaging her. I felt like I was living in hell.

Lin Yi was not a convincing actor. She was incapable of dissembling her own self. In her eagerness to find an opportunity for revenge, she stopped at nothing. I was constantly mystified and provoked into anger, and when I appeared to be led inescapably toward the fate in store for me, the Elephant would suddenly intervene and rain a trunkful of water on me, stopping me in my tracks, breaking the spell.

The Elephant acted at my behest.

"Thinking that I'm going to kill someone, and that that someone is you of all people, I feel I'd rather be killed by another, by you," Lin Yi said, "You already have blood on your hands anyway. Killing once, killing ten times, it makes no difference. You will get a kick out of it as you kill more. I'm waiting."

Lin Yi's invitation was so sincere that I felt strongly tempted to accept it. Who knows, killing might be a thrilling experience, or else why would there be a need to punish the act? But I was not yet ready to take the plunge so effortlessly. As I saw it, the mutual deference between Lin Yi and me was nothing but a deferral, postponing the inevitable.

I'm sure the earliest murder weapon was the hands. Then came sticks, clubs, swords and spears, and all the rest. And finally, words that kill.

By and by we became inseparable. All defenses between us were down. There was absolute candor that flushed out all secrets. Lin Yi stopped her seduction and provocation.

She no longer minded my presence when she changed into her underwear. Sometimes she would go into the bathroom, without a word, to rub my back. Everything was spontaneous; there was no impulse or urge, legitimate or otherwise. We slept in the same bed without bothering each other. She told me she was a virgin, I told her she was no longer one. It's all the same, she said. When we were really tired, we would give each other a hug, but only briefly. Such occasions were few and far between. When I asked her for the umpteenth time the same old question about Lin Lin and Lin Yi, Lin Yi said:

"You're silly. If I knew, I'd have told you a long time ago. You're so dense."

Our life was peaceful, leisurely, and congenial. There was laughter, good-natured ribbing and ruthless self-deprecation, as well as a tacit understanding and unspoken meeting of the minds. The days rolled on, appearing to take on a permanence and immutability. For a time we truly believed it would last an eternity.

But there were also many recurring nightmares. Dreams came every night, and every dream, without exception, was a nightmare.

In the morning I opened my eyes to look at Lin Yi, only to catch her studying me with cold, confused eyes.

I concocted an ending:

At dawn I woke up with a start, and the first sight that met my eyes was Lin Yi kneeling at my side, holding a huge elephant tusk. Her ivory-toned pajamas were trembling and the sharp end of the tusk was pointed at my heart.

"What's the matter, Lin Yi?"

"How did Lin Lin die?"

"But you said Lin Lin didn't die. You said she is alive and well."

"How did she die? How?"

The hefty tusk bore down on me. I could feel the ribs in the left side of my chest cavity crowd to one side, and then I heard the sound of fracturing ribs. My heart was pressed in, forming a crater; it was racing wildly.

"Tell me!"

Running my hand along the cold ivory and her cold, ivory-colored hand holding the tusk, I told her the story. The burden lifted from my heart, from my chest after the story was told.

Lin Yi nodded.

"That's indeed what happened."

"Then kill me, Lin Yi."

"I'll kill…"

"Kill me, Lin Lin! Do as I say."

"I'll do as you say—"

I watched the immaculate tusk bear down and plunge into my chest. Blood splattered on her hands, her face and her pajamas. The alabaster tusk was now tainted. My heart felt the cool smoothness of ivory and I died almost instantly.

I was nailed to the earth.

Lin Yi lay down beside me, speechless, her beautiful eyes wide open.

My friend the Elephant walked over, briefly paying his respects, and began throwing dead twigs, repeatedly, burying me, already dead, and her, still alive. The huge tusk rose above the mound of dead twigs like a tombstone.

The red specks on the tusk composed a timeless epitaph.

ELEVEN

I've realized once again that this could be yet another ending for this story. So far there have been dozens of opportunities for the story to end, but I took advantage of none. This time was no different. Not quitting while one is ahead is a principle I've always held dear in creative writing.

I don't deserve such a virtuous and beautiful ending.

At dawn on the day following of my assassination, I woke up suddenly, wondering why I could still wake up. Lin Yi was not there. On a corner of the bed lay her neatly folded ivory-colored pajamas. In a note placed on the pile, she said she had been called away by Lin Lin. That meant I unfortunately had been spared a virtuous and beautiful death thanks to Lin Lin. After reading the note, I felt deeply frustrated: I once again had been shafted by Lin Lin.

It was clear to me that my life had been thoroughly ruined at the hands of Lin Lin.

But I had no desire to cry.

Lin Yi was gone for days. Upon close reflection, it was then that the event had been set in motion. She had brought the diaries and the letters to help me reconsider the past; it set the stage for the opening of the show. Lin Yi suddenly had undergone a transformation into a sensible person; that was another piece of evidence. But this process was too slow, too deliberate for my taste; I had a passion for the fast and furious, for being caught unprepared.

With Lin Yi gone, I felt lonely. I became one of the living dead.

Acheng evidently had already left for the

United States. I saw a photo of him; he had
gained some avoirdupois. That's what happens
to Chinese people once they switch to a Western
diet. According to news reports, he came back
for his father's funeral, but hurried back to the
US before the standard mourning period was
over. I hadn't received any letter from Hong Zi
for over a month now, nor was there any sign
that there would be any more in the future.
In her last letter she said she had been deeply
moved by the candor of a young man who had
committed every evil imaginable and yet who
had been so open that he left nothing to the
imagination. After I wrote back to her, asking
her if she was tempted by the idea of being in
the shoes of Carmen, communication dried up.
With the Shanghai International Arts Festival
season done for the year, it became even harder
to get ahold of Wen Fei. She had to appear in
so many shows, major and minor, every day,
she didn't even have time to shave her head,
much less sit in conversation with me. In my
more peaceful moments, the urge to feel her
close shaved head was strong.

The only friend I had left was the Elephant.

The Elephant didn't hold a grudge. Despite my antagonizing him repeatedly and his run-ins with my fellow humans, he didn't believe in an eye for an eye. He was concerned about my bad back and legs and often used his trunk to massage them. Those were most enjoyable moments. I showed him the bottles of medicine that I could no longer do without. I told him I'd tried Chinese traditional remedies as well as modern Western ones but that none had worked, indeed my problems had only gotten worse. I could no longer look up at the moon. The Elephant heaved a long sigh and asked what a medical doctor was. He shook his head vigorously at my explanation. He advised me to disregard appearances, to stoop low and walk on all fours. That would cure me instantly without medical intervention. I tried it. The pain went away and I felt much more limber.

"But I can't get used to this, my Elephant. Man has walked erect for tens of thousands of years."

"But you spent many more years than that

walking on all fours."

I offered him some bananas. He asked if the price of bananas had gone up again, and if so, I should hold off on buying them.

I told him I got paid for writing, and if I worked hard enough I should be able to afford the bananas.

"Are you getting paid for writing about me too?"

"Yes."

The Elephant burst into uncontrollable laughter. He found the idea of getting paid for writing a little absurd. He said I should write more so that we could feast on bananas until we got diarrhea. He believed that those who paid me banana money had gone bananas.

The Elephant was pursuing an adolescent female elephant who was just coming of age. Every time she was mentioned, the Elephant became bashful. After consulting me and seeking my approval, he took some bananas to her. His manners had improved greatly.

They were inseparable, eating together,

sleeping together and playing together. They once had a tug of war with their trunks and the female won. Elephants found kissing awkward and did not go for hugs. Instead, the two expressed their affection by rubbing their bodies together. My friend, symbolically, would briefly mount his girl's back and she did the same to him.

"She is a virgin."

"Do elephants also attach importance to that?"

"No, but I do."

"Then, my friend, trouble is brewing."

"Impossible!"

The Elephant was immersed in happiness. He was suave, and as jaunty as a cowboy of the American West. He turned a deaf ear to my portentous words. When I advised him to be more hard-nosed and realistic and to dismiss the idea of monogamy, he instantly bristled.

"My friend, don't waste your breath."

What a fool!

After an outing with his girl, the Elephant came to me for some sex education. I told him all I knew and asked him whether he needed contraceptives. I could order them for him. The Elephant said with a snort, it's so boring to be a human. He said earnestly that he was not interested in sex just yet. He wanted to wait for his girl to grow up for him. He didn't want to hurt her.

I could only nod in approval.

The Elephant got to his feet, shaking the mud from his body, and said he was leaving. He begged my indulgence. "You have loved, so you understand," he said, "If I don't go join her right now, I'm going to die."

He ran off with a bounce in his step. I watched after him, deeply worried.

My friend was evidently rebelling, but he continued to make plans for the future, seeming blissfully oblivious to the coming disaster.

The Elephant was tender with his girl. He behaved himself extremely well, chivalrous and gentlemanly, yet very much an animal of the jungle. His girl rewarded him with coquettishness and lighthearted joy.

Responding to the suggestive teasing of the many female elephants in the herd, the Elephant howled at the sky in frustration. When it became unbearable, he would wade into the river glum-faced, trying to cool himself off with the help of the river water. He waited stoically for his girl to become an adult for him.

Since the creation of the first elephant, there perhaps had never been as unconventional a young couple as this. They could put to shame the likes of Liang Shanbo and Zhu Yingtai, Romeo and Juliet, and other legendary lovers. I was deeply moved. I said to the Elephant I planned to revise his history by expunging his affair with the middle-aged female elephant. The Elephant emitted a loud snort to show his disdain, saying that only humans were capable of such revisionist games. He declared that elephants were never afflicted by feelings of remorse. He took heroic responsibility for his actions.

I was a little ashamed of myself.

The Elephant and his girl did not whisper

in each other's ears, pass slips of paper back and forth, make mute gestures or wink at each other. They showed their affection in public, with no guilt or anxiety. They horsed around tirelessly, all day long. They would leave the herd to go on an outing, whimsically striking off in random directions and coming back only when they'd had enough fun for the day and were dead tired; once back with the herd they flopped down and went to sleep with their feet touching. Or they'd run off together into the night, with only the moon lighting their way.

The younger elephants envied them and could barely restrain themselves from following their example.

Older elephants warned them against emulating those two good-for-nothings. Behavior such as theirs would incur the wrath of the gods and the curse of their ancestors.

When they returned, they would be splattered with an assortment of bright colors that they had somehow run into, creating a sort of "punk" look. Having binged on intoxicating fruit from a grove, they staggered

about comically. The Elephant plopped down
on the wet ground and started singing, his girl
beating time with her trunk.

Of the beginning of old, Who spoke the tale?
When above and below were not yet formed,
     who was there to question?
When dark and bright were obscured, who
     could distinguish?
When matter was inchoate, How was it
     perceived?
Brightest bright and darkest dark, What was made
     from only these?
Yin and yang, blend and mix, What was the
     root, what transformed?
(From "Tian Wen (Asking Questions of Heaven),"
by ancient Chinese poet Qu Yuan, translated by
Stephen Field)

TWELVE

This story is drawing to an end. As the author, I am still undecided whether I should model it on a detective story and add a long-winded explanation at the last moment, tying up all the loose ends, to enlighten the mind and eyes of my dear reader. This is a quite useful device that will help parry complaints about the story being "too obscure and hard to understand." I recall that when the definition of the novelist was debated at some forum, someone proposed this:

A novelist is a person who tells the stories of others to others and then demands that others pay him for it.

Fortunately, I am telling my own story. I've devoted half a year, not including the time spent collecting materials, to the writing of this novel. It's been an extremely uneconomical way to go about writing a story. At this rate I am afraid I won't even be able to afford bananas. There's no profit in this, and I can already see myself getting killed in the process. I've never heard of a novelist who would sacrifice his or her life in the process of the writing of a novel. I would be the first—something I hadn't anticipated.

Nevertheless I have no intention to drug the reader. The enthralling explanation that's supposed to clarify everything and tie up the loose ends is taking forever to materialize because even I am confused. Even at this late stage, I still can't be certain whether Lin Lin is dead or alive. I still cannot tell whether she and Lin Yi are two persons in one body. Perhaps they are both illusions. What is less unclear is the unedited story about the Elephant; at least it is coherent. But I've made it clear up front that the story of the Elephant is my own concoction. I am a real flesh-and-blood person. Acheng, Wen Fei and others can attest to that. In this sense it could be said that I have been concocted by them in collusion with Lin Yi and the Elephant. I started the story with a discussion of creative writing, and I've exposed my writing process at many points throughout the story. All of this is tantamount to an admission that there is not a shred of reality in the story, which is shot through with holes and inconsistencies and loose ends.

I've written novels with fewer loose ends, such as *The Joke, Sunrise and Impressions,* and *The Story.* Writing those novels has brought in plenty of bananas.

There are stories in the world, but once written, the stories are no longer there because they lack reality.

I patted the head of Lin Yi, who existed by my imagination, and told her that without an imagination I would be an idiot. Lin Yi nodded her understanding. In this regard, we were on the same wavelength. She encouraged me to continue dreaming and fantasizing. Only don't idealize her too much, she said.

"You have a hidden agenda," I said.

Lin Yi admitted to it. Her existence depended on my continued imagination.

For a fortnight now I had a low, unexplained fever, hovering each day just below 38 degrees Celsius. This muddled up the story even more. I was still writing, but at a much slower pace. Lin Yi bought me a watermelon, which as I ran my hand over the rind reminded me of Wen Fei's shaved head. Lin Yi boasted of her expertise in picking the right melon. I believed her; Lin Lin used to plant early or first harvest watermelons. I ate the melon without saying thanks, with Lin Yi studying me. I was unperturbed; it was not in her nature to kill someone who was already half dead. So I would be safe for the moment as she awaited my recovery.

Cleaning up the rind and the seeds, Lin Yi urged me to put away the story for now; what was the hurry? She said as long as I thought of her from time to time, she would not cease to exist. As long as one was alive, que sera sera, whatever will be, will be. There was no hurry.

"Lin Yi, if I were to become incoherent as a result of this fever," I said, "I would likely lose you."

"So lose me!" she threw the rind out the window. "There will be a Lin Er, or Lin Number Two. Remember, you belong to the Lins, dead or alive. You've been marked. There's no escape for you."

These Lin girls were foolhardy enough to believe they could move mountains. I willed the story to end here. No need to ruin another girl. I had not much passion left and I'd be wise to follow the example of my one-female Elephant.

Lin Yi put away all the detective stories and mystery novels. She was reading my novel *The Color Blue*, tears streaming down her cheeks. It was a story about two lovers breaking up. I offered my manuscripts as a gift and she accepted them. I wanted to offer her some other gifts that were likely to cheer her up but couldn't think of any and so gave up.

"Stop crying, Lin Yi. Don't be like me, crying over an impossible story."

"We each cry for our own reasons. No one is like me." She wiped away her tears, "Now there is nothing to cry about."

In boredom and frustration, I exiled myself to Africa, to share in the Elephant's weal and woe. Unable to locate me, Lin Yi fired off a batch of letters to me care of the Elephant. The Elephant couldn't read, not even Arabic numbers; his race didn't have a written language. He scrutinized the letters, turning them over and over. He marveled at the plethora of human gadgets. The postage stamps intrigued him but the trouble was he couldn't read the fine print.

With a twig I traced on the ground a string of 象 characters (pronounced *xiang*, Chinese character meaning elephant), which ran the gamut of Chinese scripts from the early oracle writing to imitation Song Dynasty style. I explained in detail its pronunciation and meaning, literal and figurative, to the Elephant. When he tried the pronunciation, it sounded like "hang," to my great amusement. When I asked him to pick his favorite among the dif-

148   The Elephant

ferent scripts, he pointed with his trunk to the
clerical (official) script. So his aesthetic taste
leaned towards the Tang predilection for sup-
pleness of form. He had a very low opinion of
Lin Yi's reed-like figure, believing it to be most
ungainly. Tapping with his trunk on a photo
included in the batch of letters, he said Lin Yi
and I made a perfect pair.

An adult bull approached us at a trot, his
trunk in the air and his ears flapping. The
Elephant told me to get out of the way fast. I
could sense the hostility in the charging bull.

It was time for a showdown.

I withdrew to my home.

My back throbbed with pain. With a hand
on the wall for support, I entered the house to
find Lin Yi standing before me. She did not
offer any support but looked on as I fell like a
hollow log onto the bed. She came over to ask
if I needed a drink of water.

I requested a beer.

Lin Yi had never greeted me. I couldn't
imagine how she'd managed it. She said she

had followed Lin Lin's example. I asked what else she was trying to learn from Lin Lin. She refused to answer that question, saying only, you just wait and see.

Since the botched assassination attempt, I often had nightmares in which I'd watch my imminent execution by one of my stories' protagonist who owed her existence to me. It evoked a complex set of emotions. Lin Yi was ready, as the Chinese would say, "to kill the fish even at the risk of tearing the net in the process." Killing me would mean her own death, but she didn't mind dying with me. I told myself I shouldn't mind it either, since my punishment was thoroughly deserved.

I had no intention of negotiating with Lin Yi about our life or death.

If I were cleverer, I would find more protracted ways to put off death. All I needed to do was draw out the novel into an eight-part saga, with each part further divided into three separate volumes, until the story peters out, to be continued by some later-generation Mr. Gao E (who wrote the sequel to the *Dream of the Red Chamber*), leaving a riddle to be solved by readers and offering succeeding generations an opportunity for propitious employment. But I craved retribution.

I'd craved it ever since I loosened the grip of my numbed hands on Lin Lin's beautiful, long, slender neck.

I wanted Lin Yi to fulfill my death wish.

I offered the novel to Lin Yi for her to continue in any way she wished. Lin Yi refused, giving as her reason the fact that Lin Lin had't done this before. I said, then revise what I had written to make Lin Lin a novelist. She said, "No matter how you revise it, Lin Lin will know in her heart she has never written a novel before. You cannot impose it upon her. Why don't you clean up the mess yourself."

"Lin Yi, don't mention Lin Lin again. I'm fed up! I'm frustrated with both of you."

"The frustration is in your mind."

I said, "Lin Yi, can't you do it sooner? I can't stand it any longer. I would tear up the novel. Then you would regret not having acted sooner."

"You would rewrite it after tearing it up. As long as you live, you would always want to write it. So it would never be too late to act."

"Lin!"

"It's me."

"Lin!"

"It's me."

"Lin!"

Had it not been for what happened next to the Elephant, I don't know how things would have turned out for me that day. The Elephant was waiting for his girl to mature into an adult female; I was waiting for Lin Yi to grow stronger. It seemed she was capable of growing stronger.

Disaster struck my Elephant.

Upholding my principle of not intervening directly in any of the elephants' activities, I watched as the catastrophe unfolded, without offering a helping hand.

The Elephant and the bull five years his senior were engaged in a duel for the sake of liberty, love and ideology. The savanna was perfect for duels. They met their match in each other, one full of indignation, the other full of jealousy. Their heads lowered and trunks swung out of the way, they butted into each other repeatedly. The rest of the herd watched from the sidelines. The air buzzed with excitement, the mood festive.

The Elephant pierced the neck of the other with a tusk, sending forth a spurt of blood, briefly startling both. The wound involved no vital organs and the two rivals remained locked in battle, looking for openings to exchange blow for blow.

The Elephant's girl stood ten meters away, trembling with either excitement or fear.

My friend beat back the challenger time after time, with agile footwork, a strong trunk and tusks always pointed at the vital parts of his opponent. The bull, sapped by overindulgence in philandering, felt his strength failing him. Staggering, he was put on the defensive, his movements becoming more sluggish every moment. I was wondering if the Elephant would finish off his opponent by ending his life.

"Yaaaaa—"

The herd was furious and swarmed toward the Elephant, disregarding the millennial rules of dueling, striking him hard with their trunks. The beleaguered Elephant rushed about blindly, emitting low, desperate howls. With the blows from so many elephants raining down on him, the Elephant was soon beaten down to the ground.

The Elephant's girl bawled loudly, averting her eyes.

The bull that had been on the brink of a disastrous defeat made a sweeping gesture of acknowledgment towards the other elephants before swaggering toward the Elephant. He disdainfully slapped the Elephant's trunk with his own and spewed a thick glob of mucus on his bashed head. The rest of the herd stood in a queue to take turns pissing on him. The Elephant regained consciousness, trembling with pain.

The challenger mumbled something before raising his head in a grave air, his right tusk aimed at my friend's heart.

"Hold it!"

The Elephant's mother dashed over, warding off the trunks of the other elephants, and pushed away the malicious, yellowed tusk of the bull with her trunk. She went down on all fours and begged the herd, all her husbands, for mercy.

"Please spare his life!"

"Yaaaaa—"

The herd abandoned mother and son to themselves and returned to the jungle, singing their victory song and forcing the girlfriend of the Elephant to follow them.

The Elephant failed. He lay impotently in the grass, feeling humiliated, for his mother and for himself. He did not care about his own life. He had been the victim of a conspiracy within his herd, which mercifully spared his life afterwards. They were powerful, invincible and never feared the revenge of individuals. For elephants, that had always been the law of the land.

The Elephant opened his eyes wide, but the

damn moon was not in the sky.

He lowered his head, dejected, then stared blankly into the distance.

Suddenly, he realized that true disaster had struck. He struggled to rise to his feet and head off even if it meant risking his life. But he was restrained by his mother's trunk pressed firmly against his chest.

"My child, close your eyes as well as your ears. It will all pass."

Blood gurgled out of the Elephant's mouth.

I had to record this.

It was the night after I withdrew from Africa.

Lin Yi was beautiful and sensuous in bed. With all the light turned on, Lin Yi, bashful but fearless, undressed completely, even taking out her hairpins. She held my hands and placed them against her face, then guided them down her body, all the way to her toes. Lin Yi wanted me to take a close look at her. I looked and I saw.

"I have seen it."

"Have you memorized it?"

"I have memorized it."

"I am beautiful."

"Yes, you are beautiful."

"Then I have nothing to worry about."

With that, Lin Yi turned off all the lights. She put on her clothes and asked me to sleep on the floor and not to turn on any light before daybreak.

THIRTEEN

It was time. I went to bid the Elephant farewell.

After yet another traumatic experience, the Elephant had visibly aged and become frailer. He had a tragic look to him.

The Elephant's girl had been gang raped.

It was the idea of that sneaky, dastardly challenger. My friend was unable to do a thing because he had been restrained by his mother's trunk pressed firmly on his chest. The tragedy happened right before his eyes.

Two matronly cows trotted up to sandwich the distraught adolescent female between them and made her obey.

"I won't. I won't."

"Don't be crazy. This is the fate of every female elephant."

So the tragedy began. The ugly, lurid details, amounting to three thousands words, I once again expunged. The story resumed where the satiated bulls continued grazing as if nothing had happened. In the distance, a phalanx of adolescent females stood, every one of them shaking. The Elephant's girl, like the Elephant, collapsed into a lifeless pile on the ground. The two cows who had voluntarily become accomplices to the crime were drenched in sweat.

The young, cheery elephant couple, once so full of cherished dreams of life in the elephant world, was undeniably snuffed out.

The moon hung over Africa, indifferent to the happenings below. Kilimanjaro was shrouded in mist.

Lin Yi cried uncontrollably as she read on.

After a period of mourning, I finally thought it through and understood. I told

Lin Yi it had been inevitable. It was not a question of justice or injustice. The Elephant, a rebel against the tradition and convention of his herd, was attempting to set a dangerous precedent. It would have hastened the decline of the elephants, which were already perilously on the brink of extinction. The tragedy of the two lovers was inevitable.

Lin Yi told me to shut up. She said she would much rather see the extinction of the elephants. Beauty was the only thing worth cherishing.

That night after a bout of crying Lin Lin said with a steady voice that her face had been disfigured. She implored me not to turn on the lights.

If you still want me, you can have me. It will be my first time, believe me.

Lin Lin told me to undress, saying she was ready, at my service. She kneaded the small of my back, praying that it would be in good enough shape to enable us to consummate our union. It was so peaceful and full of passion I forgot I had a bad back.

The two female elephants helped the victim to the river and gently and with practiced ease cleaned her wound. They comforted her with their trunks, telling her that elephants, particularly the cows, must be strong. She would eventually get used to it, and when she got used to it she would feel the joy.

The Elephant's mother lifted her trunk off her son's chest, saddened over her son's misfortune. She told her son to take good care of himself while he recovered. The humiliation would pass; the important thing was to behave himself in the future, to conform. She was long past menopause and no longer had any libido. But she said with kindness that if he was bothered by the urge he could soothe it with his mother. It would be safe and less passionate, and wouldn't harm his health.

The Elephant closed his eyes in disgust before his mother finished.

His mother sobbed in sorrow.

I waited for the recovery of the Elephant, expecting that he would not let the matter rest. While waiting, I assiduously researched martial arts. I devoted a great deal of time and effort to studying the art of the "Magic Whip." I wanted to arm the Elephant, and I would gladly smuggle munitions, if he should need them. Lin Yi said she was willing to steal guns and even atomic bombs for the beautiful pair of elephants.

The Elephant shook his head, declining our offers. He said:

"The elephants are not going to reenact the tragedy of the humans."

I told the Elephant that even fighting with one's bare hands involved a lot of tricks. I demonstrated various techniques of wrestling, boxing, karate, sumo, monkey boxing, snake boxing, and Shaolin boxing. I had adapted the "nine-section chain whip" to the elephant trunk and showed him a perfectly executed routine with it.

"I won't learn it."

"Drop dead then."

The Elephant explained that once he learned the techniques he would be tempted to use them in repeated attacks and generally do as he pleased. Doing as one pleases was bad, something the elephants never did, he said.

Late that night the Elephant and his girl eloped.

Late that night I went to sleep early, exhausted. The Elephant had turned my life upside down; for him I had acquired a full array of martial art techniques, all for naught. Besides the books that filled my house, there was nothing worth stealing; so I had no potential opponent on whom to practice my skills. Now I couldn't shake off these martial arts even if I wanted to. They sorely tempted me to write kung fu novels. Late that night I had a fitful sleep. I had a premonition of something happening. I was right. I was woken up moments before dawn. I watched closely the trail often used by the elephant herd when they foraged for food. Soon I saw the two young African elephants.

"Good morning!"

"Good evening!"

After exchanging greetings with me, the

Elephant continued his hurried march, his head bent low. With his trunk he gently prodded the female elephant walking ahead of him. The female elephant looked back every few steps, apparently finding it emotionally hard to leave the herd. The two, one after the other, were on the quest for a new life along this winding trail.

I wished them well.

To elope was a beautiful thing to do.

I said to Lin Yi it was unfortunate we didn't have to elope.

Lin Yi said, soon we will.

Lying on the floor I reviewed my past. It appeared there were no regrets and that I should be content. What I lacked in life I more than made up for in my works of fiction. The Elephant was eloping in my place. I created Lin Yi and Lin Lin, and I consumed them. I consumed many an outstanding and not so outstanding personality, and myself. The legend of the graveyards of elephants was so fascinating I would donate all my organs to be able to march to such a graveyard. I would be willing to give up everything, except the pleasure of being strangled by Lin Yi. What an ending that would be! This novel would then be a posthumous work, with the name of its author in exquisite black brackets. It was the height of happiness for a writer to die by his/her own work. I would be the first to die in this fashion.

I would use the last remaining time to finish the story about the Elephant. Hopefully I'd have enough time.

The Elephant and his female companion led a happy life enjoyed by none before them and probably none after. The large amount of their mutual consumption was unprecedented. The Elephant was rosy-cheeked and high-spirited, constantly trotting even in the act of urination. However.

The female companion missed the herd.

"But they are your enemies!"

"Forgive me, dear. I have to go back."

"They will not have mercy on you."

"I will not ask for mercy."

She said it was her fate.

"I love you!"

"I love you too!"

"Don't go."

"I'll regret it when I am back with the herd. But I have no choice. Why don't you go back too? Please."

The Elephant went off in sorrow, floundering, his back turned to her.

Pregnant with the Elephant's child, the female companion went in search of her herd.

There was no way of knowing whether she eventually found her herd or if she later regretted her decision. I did not want to speculate on something I didn't know. But I knew for a fact that my friend began his roaming, his solitary peregrinations taking him to the far corners of the world. His heart must have been broken to pieces.

I tried to make him learn boxing, but he refused once again, shaking his trunk. He was exhausted by all the walking. I wanted to get him a set of video equipment to help him pass the surplus time on his hands (hoofs), but the Elephant declined, saying he was uninterested in porno videos.

One thing was certain: till his death the Elephant never took the secret path to the elephants' graveyard. The distracted Elephant had lost much of his desire and physical strength. He was bone tired. There were of course no signs pointing to possible mental illnesses. He roamed through the African jungle, as Kilimanjaro watched over him and the moon kept an eye on him. Otherwise he was of little interest to anyone.

The exquisite beauty of elephant tusks is enough to tempt anyone. He walked about absent-mindedly, hoisting an immaculate pair of tusks. Herds of elephants gave him a wide berth on the road, his bad reputation having spread to all corners of Africa. No other animal dared mess with him, and he did not mess with other animals.

In several honest talks I tried to persuade him to pull himself together. I'd just as soon see him go on a vengeful rampage, or capitulate. The Elephant would have none of that. Bound by tradition, he said that there had never been an elephant who challenged his own race. The race was always right. But he was not in the mood to return to the fold of his righteous race. The jungle was wonderful; its attraction could only be appreciated by solitary roamers. In his peripatetic travels, the Elephant lost much of his physical strength, his skin fell loose and hung in folds, his head appeared larger than ever. But the pair of beautiful tusks remained intact. He said they had lost any relevance. He was a pacifist, a conscientious objector.

He wanted me to remove the tusks as souvenirs. As he said this, he polished them with his trunk. They were 2.5 meters long and weighed about 60 kilos.

"Keep them, my friend. Don't give up on yourself so easily. Come out of your solitude a little. As you can see, I have a bad back and bad legs. I already labor under my own weight, how would you expect me to carry your tusks? Ivory looks its best only on elephants. Do you know what humans do with ivory? They make carvings on it. They could carve out an Africa on a piece of ivory as small as an ant. Take good care of your tusks. Don't let them fall out."

The Elephant said I was unbearably pedantic. He said he still considered himself happy. Happiness didn't merely mean constant laughter, nor did it consist of play. He asked me what a philosopher was. I told him that a philosopher was one who meditated on emptiness and unreality.

"Then I am a philosophical elephant," the Elephant declared solemnly.

In my view elephants have not evolved to a stage where they need to torture themselves with philosophy. Nothing will come of the philosophical musings of this elephant friend of mine. They don't have any natural enemies. That's fatal to philosophizing. Humans philosophize because they've made themselves the enemy of nature itself. But I respect his intellectual awakening. The light of reason has finally tainted the Elephant and has sowed seeds of perplexity.

"Continue your roaming, my friend. You are the most unfortunate elephant in history. You are becoming an elephant philosopher when you and your kind can't even harness fire. More glory to you. If elephants did evolve further, they would have you to thank and memorialize. They will memorialize their forefather's pure love, his search for his roots, and his philosophizing."

The Elephant told me to lie on my stomach and proceeded to give me a full-body massage. He once again touted the benefits of walking on all fours.

I did not tell him about my imminent departure from this world. What was the point? I was only one of five billion.

The Elephant walked off thoughtfully.

I watched him until he was out of sight. We would never see each other again. I didn't specialize in philosophizing and had given up the search for my roots; my love was anything but pure. So our paths diverged.

I limped towards a future without a future.

FOURTEEN

This deeply sincere story of mine is coming to an end. Chapter 14—this is the last chapter. I've run out of excuses for further deferment.

The Elephant walked deeper into the jungle. I could hear his distant singing: Of the beginning of old, who spoke the tale? When above and below were not yet formed, who was there to question? ..." This should have been the intro to this novel.

In my musings I have envisioned the Elephant's collapse in the graveyard as the ending, hoping that the Elephant's actions could serve as an edifying example for humans. Facing death with serenity, solemnity and of one's own free will has something noble about it. My Elephant was withdrawing from his herd, not to go to his death, but to embark on a quest for an immortality of the soul. The Elephant and his girl drifted away from each other, without rhyme or reason, totally ruining my perfectly good story.

The written materials at my fingertips contain many vivid and interesting stories and facts about elephants. I had considered incorporating them in altered form into the story but finally resisted the temptation. I hereby serve notice that this will not be a novel strong on pleasing the eyes. That's not what the author has intended it to be. It must be understood that no matter how pleasing on the eyes, a story about elephants has its limitations. It's Lin Lin and Lin Yi that truly please the eyes. They are as beautiful as the tusks on an elephant and therefore cannot bear the destruction of beauty.

This novel started out with a discussion of creative writing, but will not end with critical commentary. I have a profound attachment to feeling, and would abandon theory for feeling any time. This novel is full of symbolism, humans symbolizing humans, elephants symbolizing elephants, jungles symbolizing jungles, the moon symbolizing the moon, and Kilimanjaro symbolizing Kilimanjaro. In other words, everything symbolizes me. That's all.

At the end of this novel, I volunteer to march to my death in place of my friend the Elephant, even though no ivory spouts from my mouth.

I stumbled toward Lin Yi.

Lin Yi unbuttoned my clothes, took them off. As her hands passed over me, I was restored to my original form and state. The winds blew away, the river flowed on. Kilimanjaro stood indifferently.

Lin Yi said, "I am ready. I am at your service."

I rubbed my face repeatedly in her bosom and on her back. Her skin was fine and warm to the touch, a healthy complexion. She curled her long trunk around my neck. Her breasts were exquisite and elegant. I gently flogged her with my trunk, and rubbed my tusk against hers.

"Let's go into the water, into the water."

The river flowed on.

My four feet were firmly planted on the riverbed, my body and mind at ease. The arrogance of homo erectus was cast away; history was discarded. The stirrings of creation filled the loins.

Kilimanjaro kept a watchful eye.

The river water covered Lin Yi's back and she looked back at me. I took Lin Yi's tail in my mouth, my head tightly pressed against her rump. She was meek and excited. I leaned into her, my trunk holding her nape and the tip of my trunk clasping her ear on the other side.

There was no gang rape, no disfigurement of the face, and no philosophizing.

We copulated.

Afterwards, Lin Yi and I faced each other, our trunks raised and joined in an S.

We two, how long we were fool'd,
Now transmuted, we swiftly escape as Nature
    escapes,
We are Nature, long have we been absent, but
    now we return,
We become plants, trunks, foliage, roots, bark,
We are bedded in the ground, we are rocks,
We are oaks, we grow in the openings side by side,
We browse, we are two among the wild herds
    spontaneous as any,
We are two fishes swimming in the sea
    together,
We are what locust blossoms are, we drop
    scent around lanes mornings
    and evenings,
We are also the coarse smut of beasts,
    vegetables, minerals,
We are two predatory hawks, we soar above
    and look down,
We are two resplendent suns, we it is who
    balance ourselves orbic and stellar,
    we are as two comets,
We prowl fang'd and four-footed in the woods, we
    spring on prey,
We are two clouds forenoons and afternoons
    driving overhead,

We are seas mingling, we are two of those
    cheerful waves rolling over each other and
    interwetting each other,
We are what the atmosphere is, transparent,
    receptive, pervious, impervious,
We are snow, rain, cold, darkness, we are each
    product and influence of the globe,
We have circled and circled till we have
    arrived home again, we two,
We have voided all but freedom and all but our
    own joy.

Tears filled our eyes as Lin Yi and I read these lines.

I closed Walt Whitman's *Leaves of Grass* and put it aside. Then I lay flat on the bed, my haunches spread apart. It would be nice if I could be impaled by an elephant tusk right into the plank bed.

Our moon cast a sickly light on us.

Lin Yi wanted to feel my face but I deflected her hand. She felt her own face with her two hands, lingeringly.

"All right, Lin, I am ready. After this, you go find your own kind. From now on your history will be voided. You belong to the Kingdom of Animalia, Phylum: Chordata, Subphylum: Vertebrata, Class: Mammalia, Order: Proboscidea, Family: Elephantidae."

I placed her cold hands around my neck. She gave me a quick kiss before tightening her hands.

It was a clean job!

I didn't have time for a final revision. Earlier in the story I promised I would reduce the complex story to its original simplicity. I will keep my promise.

This story shall be rewritten as follows:

The Elephant
By Chen Cun

(After 14 chapters, or 44,000 Chinese characters were expunged—note by The Elephant.)

Stories by Writers from Shanghai